Forgery and Family

J. T. Berry

ACKNOWLEDGMENTS

I would like to thank my editor Laura Apger for all of her work on and improvements to this book. The cover was designed and created by Patrick Knowles, to whom thanks are also due. Special thanks go to LJB once again for all of her insights and encouragement. Her critical reading made this book much better than it would have been without her.

CHAPTER ONE

In the five months I'd officially been 'Joy D'Amico, Private Investigator', I'd seen a lot of liars, cheats, frauds, thieves, con men, and generally good-for-nothing scumbags on the make and on the take. This one was a new low. My current mark was a wayward husband named Jerry Donaldson, a corporate cog in an off-the-rack suit and an Errol Flynn mustache with delusions of glamor. In a twist to the usual story, we'd been hired by his mistress to find out if he was cheating on her too. He was.

I had to suppress a smirk when Donaldson held the door open for me. He had no idea I'd been tailing him all morning. So far, I hadn't gotten anything much worth noting, so when he'd gone into the bank, I'd followed right behind for fear of missing his withdrawal. I said, "Thank you," and smiled at him. In response, he tipped his hat.

"A pleasure for such a pretty young girl," he replied with a leer.

I had to hide my reaction a second time. This man was cheating on his wife, on his way to a rendezvous with his side-mistress, and flirting with me! I pretended to be filling out a withdrawal slip while he took out 100 dollars in small bills. As he turned around, he was still sorting it into his wallet, and I got the incriminating snapshot. A camera that fit inside a cigarette pack was every private investigator's best friend. Just one of the great toys that the war that had ended a year ago had made available to us civilians.

He left the bank and walked north. I pulled a scarf and oversized sunglasses out of my purse and followed, tying the scarf over my hair as I went. It wasn't much of a disguise, but it seemed to be enough to fool a lot of people, at least if they weren't looking out for a tail. Take away my distinctive auburn curls and apparently, I look like a different person.

Lingering half a block back, I followed my mark to a café on Sunset where he joined a slim bottle-blonde smoking an even slimmer cigarillo at an outside table. He gave her a quick kiss on the lips before sitting down, which I also snapped. He was certainly making my job easy. I took a table about ten feet away behind his right shoulder and settled in to enjoy an expenses-paid lunch. Neither of them took any notice of me. That was one advantage for the female PI. If a married man and his lover sat down together at a café table in the middle of the day and a lone man took a nearby table, it might attract their suspicion. But a single woman taking lunch or afternoon coffee was practically invisible.

Disappointingly, they lingered only long enough for salads and a cocktail. The bill came and he dropped a five dollar bill on the table. But then he hesitated, picked it up and left three singles instead. Not only unfaithful, but cheap too. Leaving behind half of my spaghetti and most of my coffee, I tracked them three blocks to a small hotel. I gave them five minutes to get upstairs before going into the lobby. A dollar was enough to get the clerk to let me snap the register where they had signed in as Mr. and Mrs. Donaldson. The creep had used his real name. Was this guy trying to get caught?

Suddenly there was a yell from the landing above me. It was Donaldson.

"Hey! What the hell are you doing there?" he shouted.

He charged down the stairs, his suit coat flapping behind

him. I ran for the door and slammed it shut behind me. Seconds later, he came barreling through. A cab was standing just a few feet away, dropping off a fare. I threw myself towards it, barging past an elderly couple who thought they'd got lucky. As I reached the door, Donaldson snatched at me, catching only my headscarf. It came away in his hand. I jumped in and the cabbie pulled away. Donaldson chased us for half a block, then disappeared in the distance behind us.

As I rode back to the office, I was flushed with exhilaration at both a job well done and a narrow escape. I made a mental note to add the scarf to my expenses. But I also felt a pang of sadness for Donaldson's wife. It had been four months since my partner Dot and I had hung out our shingle as private detectives, and in that time, a lot of our cases had been infidelity and adultery, and most of our customers had been women. No surprise, wives felt they would get a more sympathetic hearing from us. It never felt great to provide the evidence to end a marriage, but I suppose it was better for a woman to have the certainty than to live with constant suspicion eating at her.. Sometimes we helped a wife escape a bad marriage without ending up broke, which was more satisfying. And a couple of times we even had the pleasure of laying misplaced doubts to rest. This was not one of those times, but I was happy that the cheating sleazeball was going to get what he deserved. There just remained the tricky question of whether to tell his wife.

The next day was not nearly so exciting. With the Donaldson case closed, I had absolutely nothing going on. The waiting room was empty and the phones stayed mute all morning. I read the newspaper front to back and back to front, even the classifieds. I looked up at the wall for the thousandth time. The clock said 4:00 p.m. and the calendar said September 1946. When Dot and I had started out, we had known there were going to be days like this, foot-tappingly slow days that dragged like cold molasses. Days that made you repeatedly ask if it was too early to start drinking. Days where each cigarette lit the next. Days when you wished something would happen, but would probably regret it when it did. I looked up again. The clock said 4:02 p.m. and the calendar still said September.

Today aside the private investigations gig was going fine. It was just about paying its own way, even if it wasn't making us rich. We made 35 bucks a day plus expenses when we worked, and nothing when we didn't. It helped that our friend Ginnie Townsend, socialite and heiress as well as our financial backer, steered her rich friends our way. As a result, background and reference checking for potential domestic staff was becoming a specialty for us. We made a good team: Dot loved following up on their documentation, and I was happy to hit the sidewalk and talk to their references. She was the sober, strait-laced partner—the one who kept the books straight and the paperwork filed and the business above water. Mind you, she also came with a few surprises, like her talent for lock-picking.

We were also getting work from other small agencies around town. Like the Donaldson case showed, there were jobs that women could do that a man couldn't, and I don't just mean tailing somebody into the ladies' room. I'd even gone undercover for one job, posing as a domestic to figure out who was spreading malicious gossip about their employer. There were a lot of reasons the Pinkertons had an entire women's division.

I sighed impatiently and looked over at Dot. She was dealing with the tedium in her own way, but I thought I might kill her if she sorted the filing cabinets one more time. Or sharpened her pencils again. To my relief she'd pulled a thick book of the shelf and was now well into it. Dot was so much better at killing time than I was, possibly because she'd had a lot of practice when she had been running her bookstore. She didn't seem to mind spending time inside her own head. I was the opposite. I'd always been accused of being impatient, but really, I simply didn't have any ability to sit around doing nothing. When I had been driving a cab, I had never had the ability to stay still. Even when I didn't have a fare, I would cruise around looking for one, or join the line at a taxi rank and gossip with the guys. I still joined the guys for drinks from time to time, but it was getting harder the longer I was away from the job. More and more of the drivers were people I didn't know from my time behind the wheel.

Before that gig, I was flying B-17s as a ferry pilot. Now that was moving. And it wasn't just the speed. The time between takeoff and landing was an escape from everything and everybody. The plane was its own self-contained world, one where I was completely in control. At just 10,000 feet, the horizon is over 100 miles away in every direction. Down here, I couldn't see more than 10 feet, blocked by an unyielding brick wall. In the air it was just me, the plane, and the weather. Down here, there were a thousand responsibilities. I figured the chances of my ever getting to fly again were zero, unless I struck it rich and bought a plane of my own. With the war over, the air force didn't want female flyers any longer, and no airline was going to put a woman in the cockpit with so many returning veteran pilots looking for work.

I came back to Earth. The paint on the walls, which Dot had told me was called 'eggshell blue', was supposed to be calming, but it wasn't working on me. I puffed out my cheeks, abruptly pushed my chair back from my desk, stood up, and announced I was going for a walk. Dot looked up, nodded distractedly, and went back to her book. I was wrangling my way into my leather flight jacket when the bell on the outer door announced a visitor.

"This one's yours, kid," I said.

"Could you show them in on your way out?" Dot asked. Our budget very much did not cover a receptionist, so we took turns answering the door and welcoming visitors.

"Sure," I said. I opened the office door to our potential client just as she was about to take one of the half dozen stiff-backed chairs that made up our waiting room. She looked at me timidly. She was about 5'7", a couple of inches taller than me, with limp blonde hair falling straight to her shoulders and startling green-blue eyes verging on turquoise. Her skin was perfectly smooth, pale, and as clear as water. She was slim as a pencil, with almost no figure to speak off. Somehow, she seemed to shrink into herself, occupying less space than even her small body should.

She was wearing a plain, butter-yellow cotton dress with a pleated skirt, white nylons, and sunflower yellow shoes, none of which looked good on her. Overall, the getup gave her white skin a cast of jaundice. She was also wearing gloves, despite the warm Fall day, and not a single piece of jewelry, besides the simple studs in her ears. She took off her impractical little Robin Hood hat and kneaded it nervously with both hands.

Everything about her screamed "trouble" to me. This gut feeling wasn't private investigator's instincts, I was too new at the game to claim that. It was taxi driver's instincts: she was the kind of woman who would ask to be taken to the railway station, then break down crying after three blocks, telling me to turn the cab around and take her back where I picked her up. And then the tip would be lousy. I even once had a bawling fare like that who refused to pay at all, because I hadn't really taken her anywhere.

"Are you Miss D'Amico?" she asked tentatively.

I flirted momentarily with denying it and taking my walk.

"I am," I confessed. "But I was about to leave. Can my partner Miss Stone help you?"

"No," she replied, in her quivering little voice. "It has to be you, I'm afraid."

I suppressed a sigh. "Come through to the back," I told her. "And you can call me Joy."

She held out her hand and gave me a handshake as limp as a dead bouquet. "Lisa," she said.

I showed her in and indicated one of the chairs in front of my desk. She nodded to Dot, who acknowledged her in return, then swept her skirt neatly underneath herself and perched on the edge of the seat. Dot's desk was perfectly neat as always. She would tidy up the sand on the beach if you let her.

While I hung up my flight jacket, Lisa arranged her hat, gloves and purse evenly spaced along the edge of my desk. She sat stiffly upright in her chair, as though afraid to crease the back of her dress. Her feet were together and her hands in her lap. I'd never seen anybody act so prim in my life. Everything about her made me think of finishing schools, except for her clothes. Basic as they were, she wore them like she was borrowing them—or as if she needed to wear the same dress again tomorrow. I sprawled in the chair behind my desk. Dot would tell me later that I looked unprofessional, but right then, I didn't care.

Dot brought over a cup of coffee, which Lisa took carefully with both hands. Then she retreated to her own desk and pretended to be interested in some paperwork. Lisa carried the saucer to within an inch of her lips before lifting the cup and sipping so daintily she barely parted her lips. She drank like she'd once been beaten for spilling a drop and had resolved to never spill another. By some miracle of modern cosmetic science, her lipstick left no trace on the rim of the cup. She set the cup down precisely on the corner of my desk, barely causing a ripple in the hot liquid. I watched the whole performance in fascination.

"What can I help you with?" I asked when she was finished.

"I'm trying to locate my father," she replied.

"Well, either one of us could do that. Is there a reason you asked specifically for me?" I replied, my forehead furrowed.

"Because he's your father too. My full name is Lisa D'Amico."

I sat up straight, wide-eyed. Dot stared across at us. I'm

not sure who was more surprised, myself or her. I hadn't given a thought to my father in years, and I had absolutely no wish to do so now. I raised my eyebrows as far as they would go and puckered my mouth. "I think I would know if I had a sister," I said. I didn't even try to hide my irritation.

"Half-sister, actually," corrected Lisa. That didn't help my mood. I knew next to nothing about this woman and already I disliked her. I was ruffled that she'd make such a claim, which I didn't believe, and was angry at her for dropping it on me like that. And above all, for making me remember him. If she'd deliberately planned to start our relationship badly, this was the way to do it.

"Excuse me if I'm a little surprised," I said. "We could barely look less alike." Dot had once described my looks as all-Italian, curves and dark hair and olive skin. I'd take that. Lisa on the other hand was an angular ice queen.

"I guess you both take after your mothers," Dot threw in. I assumed it was supposed to lighten the mood, but nobody smiled. Dot really shouldn't try to make jokes.

"Your father left you when you were young, yes?" said Lisa, ignoring Dot's comment.

There was probably nothing I wanted to talk about less at that moment than my father. I had few memories of him, but what little I did recall was bad. Even when he was still living with us, he mostly made himself scarce. My mom later told me that it was because he was working hard to take care of us, but my grandma said he always had some foolish, possibly illegal, get-rich-quick scheme going. I must have been seven or eight before I properly understood that most of the other kids at school had fathers who were around all the time.

Raising me as a single mother on a Depression-era farm was a hardscrabble life for my mother, yet she constantly forgave my father and would not hear a bad word spoken about him. I was almost as mad at her for that as I was at him for leaving.

"Yes," I said stiffly. "I was five. What about it?"

"He came to Los Angeles and married again."

"I don't think so. He never divorced my mother."

"Be that as it may, my mother certainly has a marriage certificate. He had a child with my mother, and true to form, left when I was 13. I don't mean to be rude about him, but these are the facts."

"Don't worry about it," I said. "I don't hold onto any fantasies about what a great father he would have been if only he'd stayed. He probably did me a favor by leaving."

Dot interjected again. "He must have left more than five years ago. Why start looking for him now?"

Lisa twisted in her seat to address Dot, still keeping her hands in her lap. "Eight, in fact."

I tried to assemble a timeline in my head. That made Lisa 21, and I was just 26. Lisa must have been born very shortly after my father abandoned us. Her mother might even have already been pregnant when he left. There was a story there that I would probably never know, and I almost certainly didn't want to. It would be one more betrayal, and one more twist in my guts the next time I had to think about him.

Dot came out from behind her desk and positioned a chair next to Lisa, turning it to face her, so that Lisa wouldn't have to keep twisting to look at her.

Lisa picked up her story. "My mother died about half a

year ago. She never made any kind of will, and frankly, she didn't have anything worth leaving anyone. Except for one thing. In a letter she left for me, she explained that there was a deed to a certain property that belonged to my father. She had been holding it for him until his return. Now it was mine to look after, until he turned up. Honestly, I can't understand why she hadn't divorced him for abandonment years ago and taken it for herself. I suppose she retained more affection for him than I did. Against all reason, she must have believed that he'd come back someday."

I silently reflected that there was no explaining the things people did in family relationships. Somehow this useless, lazy, dishonest man had two wives pining for his return and two daughters who had no time for him. Maybe there were more of us, who knew. It was starting to sound like a pattern.

"Anyway," she continued, "I certainly don't feel the same loyalty my mother felt. I talked to a lawyer about what I needed to do to take possession of the property, and he said that I would need to have my father declared legally dead. In California, the main requirement for that is that he hasn't been heard from for seven years, I learned."

"It's been eight, so that's taken care of," Dot pointed out.

"Yes, but that's only part of it. There also has to be a reasonable effort to trace him. And I have no idea how to go about such a thing."

"And that's what you want us to do," I said.

"Yes. Either find definitive proof of his death, or document enough effort to satisfy a judge. Frankly, the former would be my preference."

Mine too, I thought.

"That still doesn't explain why you want me of all people," I said.

"I agree," Dot said. "It seems to me it would make more sense to pick somebody who could be objective about the whole situation. Or someone who wouldn't be so disturbed if he turned up alive," she added with a worried glance across at me.

Lisa bit her lower lip and looked down. It was the first time I had seen a crack in her icy exterior. I half-expected her to cry a little. Although if she had, a part of me would have suspected she was faking it.

"The thing is, I can't afford to pay an investigator," she said, "so I need somebody with some other incentive to help."

"And what, I should do this out of some lingering affection for my absent father? Or maybe because I want to make sure the rat is dead?" I asked.

"Of course not," said Lisa, looking up again. She hadn't managed to squeeze out a tear. "I was merely hoping that you would sympathize with my situation, given our shared history. And if I am able to get ownership of the property, I can pay you 10 percent of whatever I make when I sell it. I think I can get 10,000 dollars for it. Does that sound fair?"

I still felt unsettled. There was some kind of catch here, but I couldn't figure out what it was. "What kind of property are we talking about?"

"It's an empty lot in Century City, about three acres in size. I guess it wasn't much when he bought it. Much of that area was still open land at the time, but now, I think either of the studios that neighbor it would pay a decent amount of money for it. Space is at a premium over there and undeveloped land is rare. Of course, nobody has been able to buy it because they can't find the owner."

If the stories my grandmother had told me were true, it was unlikely my father had bought it at all. It was much more likely he had won it in a crooked poker game. My mother and my grandmother had very different views on the worth, or worthlessness, of my father. For my mother, he was the only man she had ever loved, and nobody else would ever live up to her adolescent fantasy of him. For grandma, he was a schemer, a scammer, a worthless drinking and gambling layabout, who was probably unfaithful too. She thought he had ruined her daughter's life and that he'd do more good in the ground as fertilizer than he ever did while breathing. I was inclined to side with grandma.

I pushed my chair away from the desk and leaned back. I lit a Lucky Strike, took a long draw, and blew the smoke out, more to buy time than because I needed one.

"So we find the proof of death, you sell the lot, we get paid out of the proceeds? That's the proposition?"

"That's the size of it," said Lisa.

"And if we find he's still alive we get nothing for our trouble."

"Until he eventually dies, yes. You'll have to decide if you're willing to risk having to wait a bit longer to get paid."

"There's one other potential scenario to consider," said Dot. "Suppose we do turn up nothing and you go to court to get him declared legally dead. I'm not a lawyer, so I don't know whether the official date of death will be when the ruling comes down, or seven years from when you last heard from him."

"What difference does it make?" asked Lisa.

Her tone was a little petulant, it seemed to me.

"If it's seven years, you're in the clear," Dot said. "Ownership passed to your mother as next of kin when he officially died, and now it has passed to you. You'll just have to endure the tedious probate process. But if it's the date of the ruling that matters, then officially, she died first. Therefore, the deed still belonged to him when he was declared dead."

"So?" said Lisa. An impatient tone was definitely there that time.

"So then half of the property would belong to Joy, since she's equally his daughter."

I adored Dot's logical mind. I never would have thought of that angle.

"Oh, right," said Lisa. For a moment, she looked as devastated as if Dot had told her that her dog had died. But then she recovered. "Well, I suppose half of 10,000 dollars is still better than nothing. And it'd be a bigger payout for you. Do you think it can be done?"

"It's possible," I said. "We've got a better chance if he stayed here in LA. If he moved somewhere else, it could be really hard."

Dot looked at me. "It's a risk. We might have to turn away other work for this, and we're not exactly flush ourselves," she said. She didn't look keen, and I wasn't convinced about the project either.

"Dot and I need to talk about it," I told Lisa. "Can you come back tomorrow this same time? We'll give you a decision then."

Tomorrow would be Saturday. We wouldn't normally open the office, but I didn't want a decision on this hanging over us all weekend.

"Very well," she said.

"Where can we reach you if we need to?" Dot asked.

Lisa paused. "For the moment, I'm staying at the Belvedere in West Hollywood. But there's no phone in the room."

"Can we leave messages at the desk there?"

"I suppose so. Just tell them room 207."

We showed Lisa out and then watched from the window as she hailed a cab. As it pulled away, Dot and I exchanged glances. By silent agreement, we closed the office for the day and walked over to Jack's bar.

Jack himself was behind the bar that afternoon and he had our drinks on the counter before the door closed behind us—a beer for me and straight rye for Dot. She'd given up trying to teach him how to make a Manhattan. Jack's place had been my regular bar when I'd been driving cabs, and I'd introduced Dot to it the very first day we met. It hadn't taken long for the bar to adopt her, and she had quickly gotten over her first reaction to a spit and sawdust working men's drinking hole.

We perched ourselves less than elegantly on stools at a high top, clinked glasses, and lit up cigarettes. Kool for her and Lucky Strike for me.

"That must have been quite the revelation for you," said Dot. "How much of her story do you believe?"

"Well, she knows about my father leaving me, so that's

one thing," I replied. "I don't know where else she could have known that from. As for the rest, it sounds cockeyed, but why make it up if it isn't true? It seems a long way round to go, just to get free investigative services. And there's no reason I can think of for her to go looking for my father if it isn't true."

"Yes, it's an unlikely story on its face. If I were going to make something up, I'd pick something simpler. But I would like to see some proof of her identity. And how do you feel about the prospect of investigating your own father?"

"Conflicted. Like I said, I don't have many memories of him, but I do have a lot of resentment for what he did to my childhood. And for what his leaving did to my mom. I don't know that I want all of that dredged up again."

"That's fair enough. I'm certainly not going to push you to do anything you're not comfortable with. And you definitely don't look comfortable right now."

Dot is not the best at reading people's emotions, so for her to say that, I must have been positively radiating discomfort like a nun at a burlesque show.

I took a swig of beer and a pull on my cigarette, and then tried to shrug the tension out of my shoulders that I hadn't even realized I was carrying. "You're right, but walking away might be worse. Now that I know half the story, I think I need to know the rest. And I feel like I owe it to my mother too. Maybe confirming Lisa's story might be what it takes to break the spell my father has on her. Especially if he's dead now. Incredible as it sounds, my mother still pines for him."

"He must have been some kind of charmer. And there's the other thing. How do you feel about the possibility of a little inheritance?" she continued.

"I'm not going to say no if it's there, but I'm not convinced it even exists. And if it does, it would be half of 10,000 dollars, minus the legal expenses it takes to go through probate, whatever that leaves. It would be nice, but it's not going to be life-changing. I'm also worried the whole thing might be a con of some kind," I said.

"Perhaps. If she asks us to front her money for expenses, then definitely."

"I'm thinking a classic pigeon drop, maybe." I took a large swig of beer.

"What is that?" Dot asked, her brow furrowed.

"It's a con where you trick somebody into paying a lot of money for something that turns out to be worthless. Suppose we get the proof we need for her, or both of us, to take ownership of the deed. Then she gets a buddy to pretend to be willing to pay a high price for the property once probate has been settled. She pleads poverty, saying she can't wait for the courts, so she asks me to buy her out, saying I can get it at a bargain price if I pay her cash now, and sell it on at a big profit later. Then she disappears with my money, the alleged buyer is suddenly nowhere to be found, and the deed turns out to be worthless. Something like that. She might think it has a lot more chance of working on me than on some random stranger."

Dot nodded. "It might work even easier for her if it turns out you already own half, so you're motivated to take over the whole thing. And she's already set up the poverty plea with her story about not having money to pay us."

"If that's the sting, she's going to be out of luck. I don't have any money either," I replied.

"A couple of other things also bother me," Dot said. "One, she took a taxi from outside the office."

"So?"

"That seems extravagant for somebody too broke to pay us, don't you think?"

"Yeah, that is off. The Red Line is only a couple of blocks away."

"And there's her demeanor, too. She was very stiff the whole time. She didn't even smoke. It reminded me of some of the girls I knew at college. The aspirational would-be debs from middle class families who'd been through deportment classes and only wanted to socialize with girls richer and more socially connected than themselves. And with the boys of course, when we had dances. They could never let on where they really came from. Maybe it doesn't mean anything, but it felt like she was trying really hard not to give away anything about herself."

"I got that too. She was totally buttoned down, and careful about everything she said or did. And there wasn't exactly a 'long-lost sisters reunion' mood from her, either. It was all business."

"The biggest thing that worries me here is you. If it's a con and she's playing on your emotions, I don't want to see you get hurt," Dot said. She reached across the table and put her hand on top of mine. Even though she was a couple of years younger than me, she would try to Big Sister me from time to time. I didn't always mind.

"If you think we should turn this down, you can say so," I said. "But I think I want to at least check out her story a little first."

"Okay, but let's proceed with caution. Do you know anything about the Belvedere?"

"Not much," I said. "I've dropped people there when I was driving the cab, but I've never been inside. From the outside, it's definitely not the Marmont, but it ain't no dive either."

"I'm surprised the rooms don't have phones. Isn't that quite commonplace these days?"

"I only know hotel rooms from what I see in the movies, but it seems like it. If that was a lie she made up on the spot, it makes me wonder what she's covering for."

"Maybe we should look it over," Dot suggested. "See how expensive it is, what the clientele looks like, and ask some questions. It might fill in some background for us."

"We could go over there tomorrow morning, before she comes back to see us," I said.

"Let's meet at the office at nine and ride over," replied Dot.

It sounded like a plan. Some of our cabbie friends had started to drift into the bar, so with the decision made, we joined their table and put work worries out of our heads.

Chapter Two

The Red Line dropped us a block away from the Belvedere and by 9:30 a.m, we were standing in front of a modestly-imposing, gray brick building in the middle of a busy shopping street. Fake pillars and stone veneers around the windows dressed it up a little, although it was nowhere near as upscale as the Beverly Hills Hotel or some of the others over on Wilshire Boulevard. You probably wouldn't see Rita Hayworth coming in and out. Still, it also didn't look like the kind of economy hotel that somebody watching every penny would choose. I could have recommended three or four cheaper places in walking distance that weren't exactly flophouses.

The glass and brass door didn't have a doorman anywhere to be seen, so we let ourselves in. The door opened on to a large lobby with a high ceiling that was supported by rich wooden columns. There was an extravagant chandelier in its center and sconces along the walls. It put me in mind of the lobby of the better kind of theater. Around each column were banks of red velvet-covered bench seats, some of them occupied by businessmen who were mostly sitting alone, reading newspapers and smoking. It seemed to be an unwritten rule of businessmen in hotels to completely ignore each other, everywhere from the bar to the lobby to the restaurant.

The design had been stylish before the war, sleek with lots of chrome and curved wood instead of corners, but was a little corny these days. 'Streamline Moderne,' Dot told me it was called. Directly across the lobby from the doors was a wide staircase, and next to it, two elevators with elaborate bronze cage doors decorated with geometric motifs. Operators in gold-braided coats were standing by. To our right stood a concierge stand, unmanned for the moment, and beyond that a stall selling newspapers, cigarettes, and candy, as well as a few other sundries. Taking up the wall to our left was a long counter of the same heavy wood as the columns. Behind it stood three clerks, two women and a man, wearing matching blazers and smiles. At first sight, it certainly looked more like a businessman's hotel than a tourist one, and a decent quality one for businessmen with expense accounts, not traveling salesmen who'd watch every penny and share a room, or even a bed, with a stranger. Although I felt uncomfortable in the suit I was wearing, I was glad Dot had asked me to dress up a little. We wanted to be mistaken for customers, not cab drivers.

"Let's split up. If you can go and ask about room rates, I'll see if the desk knows anything about Miss Lisa D'Amico. Join me over by the newsstand when you're done," I told Dot.

Dot headed off to the nearest of the three clerks, and I approached the woman at the far end. She was tidy-looking, well-groomed, no wedding ring, and somewhere around 40, if I had to guess. I also guessed this wasn't her idea of a great career, but still better than selling perfume in Bullock's. Now that the war was over and the men were home, options for working women were somewhere between slim and none.

"Good morning, how can I help you?" she asked. Somehow, she managed to greet me without changing her smile.

"Hi, I'm looking for a friend of mine. I was supposed to meet her here, but I don't see her in the lobby."

"And she's staying with us, I presume?"

"Yes. Miss Lisa D'Amico. She arrived in the last couple of days."

She opened a large ledger and ran her perfectly manicured finger down a list of check-ins from yesterday, then flipped back to the day before and then the day before that.

"I'm sorry, I'm not seeing anybody by that name," she told me. "Would you like me to go further back?"

"She should be in room 207," I said.

She paused and frowned at that. She pulled a clipboard out from a shelf under the counter, and flipped the pages attached to it until she found the one she needed. "I thought so. 207 is a double, and there is a couple staying there. No Lisa D'Amico."

"Oh," I replied. "Maybe I made a mistake about the hotel. Is there another Belvedere?"

"Not here in West Hollywood. There is one in downtown Los Angeles and we occasionally get their phone calls by mistake, but it's much larger and more expensive."

I thanked her as politely as I could and wandered off to the newsstand where Dot was waiting for me. She had bought a pack of Kools while she was waiting and was smoking one. She offered me one but I shook it off and pulled out one of my own Lucky Strikes instead.

"15 dollars a night for a single, 25 for a double. There are a lot of decent places cheaper than that," Dot reported. "And they do have a telephone in every room. What did you find?"

"Well, she either lied to us about her name, her room

number, or where she's staying. Possibly all three. Let's talk to that guy." I jerked my thumb back towards the desk. At the far end of it stood a large man, smoking a cigar and scanning the lobby. He was wearing a three-piece suit, the vest buttoned tightly across his gut, and his left thumb was hooked into his vest pocket. I doubted whether his coat could button. His hair looked thin, and it had been artfully combed across his pate to cover his advancing baldness, but only from a distance. I figured he was about a year away from wearing his hat indoors.

"Who is he?" Dot asked.

"House detective," I replied.

"How can you tell?"

"The way he holds himself and keeps scanning the room says ex-cop to me. Also, when I was up at the desk, I noticed he's wearing a shoulder holster."

"Perhaps this isn't such a nice hotel after all," Dot offered.

"Nah," I said. "Lots of hotels have a house dick to deal with trouble quietly, from both the guests and the staff. It's better than having cops slapping their big feet all over the lobby floor. Let's go introduce ourselves. We'll want him on our side."

Up close, he was no less stout, but he did appear taller. He was maybe six feet, seeing as Dot and I both had to look up to him. His cheeks held the red starbursts of the determined drinker and his nose looked like it had been punched several times, getting a little flatter and a little broader each time. The suit was inexpensive and a little shiny at the elbows and knees, and he was wearing yesterday's collar and cuffs. I guessed that being a house detective didn't pay that well, and

I mentally crossed it off my list of career ambitions.

"Excuse me," Dot said in her best bookshop voice, the one she used to use for customers. "Are you the house detective?"

He didn't look at us, just nodded and kept scanning the room.

"We're private investigators. I'm Dot Stone and this is Joy D'Amico." She handed him one of our cards. "As a courtesy, we wanted to let you know we're on a case here that involves one of your guests."

He looked down briefly at the card, then tucked it into his vest pocket where it could keep his thumb warm, and went back to watching the lobby. He blew out a large smoke ring through his generous lips, then looked down at us.

"Appreciate it, but I'm not sure I'm happy about the two of you working my turf," he said in a growly bass voice. "I'd ask what the case is, but I don't like being told to mind my own damn business. Just tell me it isn't trouble for me, or I'll have to ask you to take it outside."

"Thank you. And no, you're not going to have to break up a fight in your lobby."

"Okay. Keep it that way and we'll get along. Name's Lowry. Call me Sam."

"Maybe you can help us get out from under your feet. The woman we're looking for is named Lisa D'Amico," I said.

Sam stared into the distance for a few seconds. "Not ringing any bells. What does she look like?"

"About Dorothy's height, very slim, with shoulder length straight blonde hair and blue-green eyes you wouldn't forget."

"That her?"

He pointed his cigar at the door. Dot and I both turned to look, then snapped back. The door was closing behind Lisa, who was on the arm of a tall, well-built, perfectly-tanned man in a neatly tailored dark gray suit with a light gray fedora in his hand. The jacket and skirt she was wearing looked expensive. I don't know anything about high-end fashion, but it looked a lot like one of the suits Ginnie had given to Dot when she decided she wasn't going to wear it again, and Ginnie didn't wear anything cheap.

I watched in the mirror behind the counter as the two of them walked stony-faced and silent towards the elevator. One of the operators jumped to attention and opened the gate and the door for them, and they stepped inside. Lisa didn't give any sign she'd seen us. I exhaled.

"That was her," I said. "What name is she going by here?"

"Lisa Daubman. Mrs. Alex Daubman," replied Sam.

"That tracks," I said. "Conmen often stick to the same first name, or at least similar-sounding names. Makes it easier to remember. They can also play it off if they accidentally answer to the wrong name."

Sam grunted. I had no idea whether that signified agreement or the opposite.

Dot looked at me with doubt on her face. I could tell she wanted to ask whether I got that from one of the true-crime magazines I read, but she wasn't going to do so in front of a stranger.

"I don't like it when there's something hokey going on in my hotel," Sam stated flatly. His eyebrows closed together, etching deep furrows between them. His eyes were brighter. I figured we had engaged his detective's brain.

"Well, she's lying to at least one of us," said Dot.

"It might just be they're pretending to be married so they don't get grief about sharing a room," he mused. "Every hotel gets some of that, and I don't want to jump to conclusions if they're just having an affair. But we don't want to get a reputation for it, because the next thing you know, people will be bringing hookers here and signing in as 'Mr. and Mrs. Smith'. And once you have hookers, you get pimps hanging around the lobby, and they're harder to get rid of than cockroaches."

"Heck, they might even really be married," I added. "If it were me though, I wouldn't cash any checks for her."

"What do you know about Mr. Daubman?" Dot asked.

"Not much beyond what you've seen for yourselves. He's some sort of executive for one of the studios, but who isn't in this town? He carries a lot of cash and likes to impress people with it. Tips extravagantly. Dresses himself and her like they're going to fancy-shmancy social events most evenings. And my Old Cop instincts say he could handle himself in a fight. That's about it."

"One more thing, if you don't mind," I said. "See the skinny guy in the black pinstripe suit and the gray hat over by the concierge stand? Do you know him?"

"I've seen him in the lobby a couple of times in the past week," replied Sam. "Could be a guest, could be meeting somebody. What's he to you?"

"I think I saw the same guy hanging around our office yesterday afternoon. Standing across the street, propping up a wall and pretending to read a newspaper."

"Huh. He hasn't made any trouble so far, but I'll keep an

eye on him."

"Thanks, Sam. We should get out of your way now," I said.

"Thanks for the tip-off about Lisa. I appreciate you being straight with me. But make sure you check in with me any time you're working here." He offered his hand and we took turns to shake it. His mitt was so big he could have shaken both of ours at once.

Chapter Three

We regrouped back at the office. Dot arranged herself behind her desk, and I perched myself on the corner. Coffee and cigarettes in hand, we compared notes.

"Here's something I'm wondering about," I said. "She could have told us she was checked in as 'Lisa Daubman', and she wouldn't have had to give us a dumb story about the phone. It seems like an unnecessary lie to get caught in."

Dot stared off into space for a minute, her analytical mind ticking away.

"Try this. If we called and asked for 'Lisa Daubman', the hotel would connect us to the room. And then Alex might pick up," said Dot. "So maybe that's what she's avoiding. Which means she doesn't want him to know she's seeing us. It's possible he doesn't know about the property at all."

"Yeah, it's a lot more awkward if she tells us it's okay to call, but not to talk to her husband. We should be careful not to blow her secret at least until we know more about what's going on," I replied. "She might be conning him too, but there are also legit reasons she might not want him to know what's going on."

"It's possible. By the way, good call on the house detective," Dot said. "I feel like we've got another set of eyes on Lisa D'Amico, or Daubman, or whoever."

"Huh. It sounds like you don't want to just walk away from this whole business after all?" I replied.

"I confess, I'm a bit intrigued by the lies she's weaving. How do you want to handle it, though?" asked Dot.

"I want to challenge her story," I replied. "If she's telling the truth, I want to know what the deal is with my father, if only for my mother's sake. And I'm not completely cold to the possibility of a small inheritance. But if she's lying, I don't want her running around town telling stories about my family. If we press her and her story falls apart or turns into a bigger pile of lies, then I'm out."

"Fair enough," said Dot. "You know, you've never told me much about your childhood," Dot said. "Why don't you fill me in? It might be useful to know when Lisa comes back. I want to be able to cross-check whatever story she tells us."

"It's a bit messy. And bear in mind, a lot of this is what I heard from my mom and my grandparents. I didn't get it all first-hand."

Dot took out a writing pad and a pen. Somewhere along the line, she'd picked up shorthand, and she took great notes. I could do shorthand too, but often got so caught up in a client's story that I forgot to keep up with my notes. It was just one more way I envied her mental discipline.

"I told you before I was born in Nevada, right? I grew up on my grandparents' farm," I began. "My mother was very young, and she was still living with her parents when she and my father were married. According to her, they stayed on the farm because they were both too broke to afford their own place. Until I came to LA, that was the only place I ever lived."

"How old were the two of them?"

"He was 17 and she was 16."

"So both of them would have needed their parents' permission to marry, right?"

"Not my mom, no. The way she told it, a girl could marry

at 15 back then, if she wanted, with nobody's permission. This was 1920, by the way. My grandparents would've said no, she told me, because they didn't approve of the guy. But once it was done, they weren't going to put her out on the street."

"Do you know what his parents thought?"

"No. My mom never met them. He claimed they were long dead, but who knows? He had to get a judge to approve his getting married. His name was Tony, by the way. I don't think I mentioned that. My mom was Marjorie."

Dot jotted a few notes and stared into the distance a little. "So they were married in 1920… and you were born the same year?"

"July 1920. I know what you're thinking, and yes, though my mom never talked about it, there's no getting around the dates. When I was a teenager, we called it a 'short pregnancy'. That's probably one reason my grandparents came around. And why the judge okayed it too. Better than the alternative."

"And then Tony left in… what, 1925?" she asked.

" '25, yes. Crazy as it sounds, my mom has never stopped believing he'll come back, like he went out for cigarettes and is just running a little late."

"And your mom's still alive, you said."

"Alive and well and running the farm now. And on top of that, she's taking care of her parents. I write her once a month like a dutiful daughter. And twice a year, on Christmas and my birthday, I hear back that she's still kicking."

Dot looked like she was feeling awkward about where this story was going. She was always uncomfortable around other people's emotions, but we needed to get it out before we talked to Lisa again.

"You grew up on the farm, then?" she prompted. We hadn't even gotten out of my earliest childhood memories, and I needed to move it along.

"Yes, but I had zero interest in farming. Everything about it is so slow and repetitive. You plow and plant, and then you wait for months, and eventually you get crops, assuming nothing goes wrong. You pull up weeds, and a week later, the same weeds are back. You milk a cow, and the next day, you milk the same cow. And all the time, you're at the mercy of the weather and the bank."

"I can see you'd have to have a certain stoic and solid approach to really commit to it. And no offense, but that's not you," said Dot.

"No kidding," I replied. "I'm way too restless. Maybe I get it from my father. But in my town, the alternatives seemed to be shop work of some kind if you were lucky, or get married and make babies if you weren't. The only thing that ever caught my eye was the crop duster. Every time it came by, I would stand and stare and imagine myself up there, looking down and moving faster than anything on the ground. I kept nagging Zak, the owner, to take me up, and on my 13th birthday, he finally did, thinking that would be an end of it. Instead, I started nagging him to teach me to fly. I convinced him he could make a lot more money if I was flying jobs for him. Six months later, I was flying solo and dusting folks' crops. I was socking away solid money for a 13-year-old working a few hours after school and weekends. I didn't have any kind of license at first, but this was rural Nevada. Nobody was checking. "

Dot got up and refilled our cups. "Is that how you got the flying gig during the war?" she asked. She knew I'd delivered bombers from the west coast factories to bases in the east.

"It helped, for sure. And before that, it also meant I could stay in school until I was 18. We had a brand new high school building, but most of the other girls were dropping out at 15 or 16 to work on the family farm or get a job in town to help pay the bills. Some of them even got married, like my mother had. I don't know what it was like in the cities, but for us, it was still the Depression."

"Then what?"

"You remember '37, right? Things had been getting better for a couple of years, but then we had another downturn. Zak didn't have enough work for himself, let alone for me, and the farm wasn't doing great either. So I packed my savings and my clothes and took a Greyhound to LA, where they said things weren't as bad." I laughed. "Seeking my fortune in the big city, I guess."

"Okay, that brings us up to age 17, if my timeline is right," Dot continued.

"Yeah, 17. So I lied about my age and found an apartment in LA with some other girls, and learned to type and file and did secretarial work for an insurance company, which by the way, is the most boring thing possible. After a while, they put me on the receptionist desk, which was a bit better, because at least I got to talk to people. And then the war came, and the rest you know."

She put her pen down. "When Lisa gets here, I'm going to play dumb about all this if it comes up. That'll give me an excuse to ask the questions you won't be able to ask, and see if I can find any inconsistencies."

"Makes sense," I said. "How do you want to play the business from the hotel this morning?"

"Keep mum. Don't let on we were there or know anything she didn't already tell us. That's an intelligence advantage for us, and we don't want to spook her. That's the way I learned it in the Army."

Possibly the most improbable fact about Dot was that she'd worked in Intelligence during the war as a codebreaker, a secret shared with just myself and Ginnie. Although anybody who knew her well would agree she had the perfect brain for it.

That left nothing but the waiting. I opened up one of the true crime magazines I was constantly reading, and Dot cracked a law primer. She was the only person I had ever met who read law books for the fun of it..

Chapter Four

The day was broken up by a job that came in. A friend of Ginnie's suspected that one of her staff was stealing from her—small pieces of silverware and possibly cash—and wanted us to find out who was doing it. It was a routine process for us by now: We would do background checks and follow them on their days off to see who was visiting pawn shops with a full bag and leaving with an empty one, or spending more than they should. I didn't feel great about these kinds of jobs when they ended with somebody getting fired, and occasionally even prosecuted, but I told myself that at least we were ensuring the right person was blamed and the others were exonerated. It was work Dot could easily fit in around wherever this other business led us.

Around three, a cab pulled up outside, and a few moments later, the bell on the door announced Lisa's arrival. She was wearing a cheap-looking floral print dress, a big step down from the outfit she had been wearing at the Belvedere. It didn't suit her any better than the yellow one she had worn the day before.

We waited for her to come through to the office. As soon as she stepped inside, Dot and I stood up and looked at each other, our faces mirroring concern.

"What happened to your eye?" Dot asked.

Lisa had done her best to cover it with heavy concealer, but there was a very obvious green and blue bruise circling her left eye. Skin as pale as hers made it impossible to hide.

"Oh," said Lisa, a little tremulously, "it's nothing. I bumped into a door."

Dot and I looked at each other again. She knew what I was thinking, and she nodded her agreement.

I sat her down at my desk and Dot sat next to Lisa. I waited for her to meet my gaze.

"I'm going to be completely blunt with you," I said. "Neither of us believes that. If you can't come clean with us about what's going on, we're not going to be able to help you."

She lowered her eyes to her lap and made the same almost-crying face I'd seen yesterday. I was even more convinced she was faking it. She looked up.

"This is absolutely confidential, yes?" she asked.

"Of course," I replied.

"Obviously this wasn't an accident," she said, gesturing to the black eye. "I've been playing the horses and had a streak of bad luck. I owe money to a bookie and I'm late paying him. If I can get the money for the property, I can pay him back and have plenty left over."

"You realize it could take months for you get title to the property, even if we can prove it's yours?" said Dot.

"Yes, but I'll deal with that when I have to. Maybe I can give the deed to the bookie as security?"

Dot and I exchanged looks again. That sounds like a setup for the pigeon drop con we'd talked about earlier, I thought.

"There's one more thing that's bothering us," she said. "You're staying at a decent hotel and riding in taxis. How can you afford that?"

Lisa was silent for a few moments. I guessed she was calculating how much of a lie she could get away with.

"I left something out when I first came to talk to you. I

have a boyfriend, his name's Alex. He's putting me up at the hotel until I can get an apartment, and helping me out with a little cash. But he can't know about any of this. I'm afraid he'll demand a share if he finds out, and there's little enough in this for me as it is."

"Would you mind stepping into the waiting room for a minute?" said Dot. "Joy and I need to talk." Lisa gathered her things, stood up and went out. Dot closed the door behind her.

"What do you think?" I said.

"I liked her first lie better," replied Dot.

"Yeah, me too. I wouldn't have believed that story if it had come out of George Washington's mouth. That's always the problem with lies, isn't it? You pile one on top of another until the whole thing comes tumbling down."

"Do you want to send her away?"

"Most of me is screaming 'yes', except for one thing. That black eye says she's really in trouble, even if it's not the trouble she claimed. And there's a part of me that doesn't want to turn away from that. So I think I have to stay with it and see how it plays out a bit longer. But that doesn't mean you have to be dragged in."

"Don't worry. If you're in, I'm in. I do have one condition though."

"What's that?"

"If real paying work walks through the door, I'm going to take the job and you'll be working this alone while I take care of it. We're not making so much money that we can afford to have neither of us getting paid this week."

Dot brought Lisa back into the office and we gathered

around my desk as before. I let Dot lead.

"We're willing to spend some time on this," she said, "but we'd like to see some validation. Do you have anything to confirm your identity?"

"I thought you would ask," replied Lisa, "so I came prepared." She opened her purse, dug around a little, and pulled out a small card and a folded piece of paper.

Dot took them. "Driver's license and a birth certificate," she said. The license was a little dog-eared and the birth certificate was creased twice, where it had been folded in thirds. She held the certificate up to the light, examining the watermark. 'Vital Record' was printed across the top and 'Certified Copy' across the bottom, and there was an official-looking stamp in the corner. "What about the deed?"

"I didn't bring that. It's in a safe place."

"Bring it next time. I'm curious to see it." Said Dot. She took the papers over to her desk and pulled a jeweler's loupe from her top drawer. Plugging it into her eye, she peered critically at both the license and the certificate. Then she rubbed the paper of the certificate between her thumb and forefinger. I had no idea whether she actually knew how to detect a fake, or whether she just wanted to see if the performance made Lisa anxious. It didn't. Our would-be client had resumed her regular Sphinx-like calm.

Dot handed the papers back to Lisa, who buried them deep in her bag. Dot went over to the filing cabinet and pulled out a folder. It had D'AMICO written across the top in blocky capitals. "I took the liberty of writing up a contract. Look it over and if you're happy, sign at the bottom."

"Do we really need to be this formal?" said Lisa.

"I'm afraid so," said Dot. "It's a licensing requirement. We can't take any compensation without a contract. But in any case, it protects us both. It gives you rights of confidentiality, and it indemnifies us if you mislead us into doing something illegal."

I had no idea whether any of that was true, but Dot sounded very convincing when she put on her bookshop voice. And the lawyer Ginnie kept on retainer had drawn up a standard contract for us to use, so maybe it was true.

"That last part sounds like you don't trust your customers," said Lisa, archly.

"It's more of a precaution. In this business, clients sometimes want us to do things that are, to put it nicely, questionable. This allows us to tell them that if we do, it's on them, not us."

Lisa read through the whole contract, which most of our clients did not do. It set out what our assignment was—to conduct a search for Tony D'Amico—and specified that we got paid a percentage of the value of the deed. Except of course, we weren't getting paid if we found him alive. When she had finished, she signed at the bottom and handed it back to Dot. She signed it too and passed it over to me for the final signature.

"Okay, now we're in business," said Dot. "So, tell us everything you can about Mr. D'Amico."

"Well, the last time I saw him was eight years ago, like I said yesterday. He and my mother had been fighting a lot, so—"

I flinched. "Physically?" I interrupted.

"Oh, not at all. Just words."

That didn't calm me at all. I'd grown up with a grandfather who always seemed on the cusp of violence, even if he only ever raised his voice to me and not his fist. Often, he seemed most dangerous when he said nothing at all. Even now, raised voices immediately made me cold and hard inside, ready to fight or run. My mother had not been so lucky. She'd had to learn the hard way not to talk back, and up until the day I left, she still tensed up when his face became dark, and I'd had to watch in helpless fear more than once as he struck her. Maybe that was why I was such a sucker for Lisa's story. My mother had protected me, threatening to leave if he hurt me, but nobody had protected her. Not after my father left. It occurred to me that his failure to protect her was a big part of my resentment towards him. I dragged myself back to the conversation and tried to focus.

"Anyway, the fighting had been getting worse, and then one day, he calmly told my mother—they were inside, and I was listening from the yard through the window—that it would be better for both of them if he moved out. She agreed. He promised he would send money for our upkeep, so she wouldn't have to worry about going to court."

"And did he?" I asked.

"For the first few months, money orders came in the mail most weeks, although not in regular amounts. I imagine he was sending whatever he could afford. And then one day, they stopped and we never heard from him again."

"I don't suppose you have any of the envelopes?" asked Dot.

"Actually, I do. My mother kept most everything that connected her to him," she said. "So I hung on to them too, just in case. There's maybe two dozen all together."

Lisa fished around in her purse again and pulled out a stack of yellowed envelopes with worn corners, tied together with twine. She handed it across to Dot who flicked through them, and laid out half a dozen on the table. They were all addressed in a clumsy, uneven scrawl to Emma D'Amico at a Claremont address, and Dot made a note of it. The postmark was Central LA, but the return address said simply Tony D'Amico at General Delivery. Lisa held out her hand and Dot handed them back.

"The address on the front here, was she still living there when she passed on?" said Dot.

"Yes, and I stayed there for a few months afterwards, but I had to move out," replied Lisa. "The lease had been paid up through the end of last month, but I couldn't afford to renew it. In any case, once my mother died, I didn't want to live there. Honestly, there was no reason to. It was a dump. I packed up my few things and anything that looked like important paperwork, and then I left the rest of her belongings. There was really nothing worth taking or selling. I've been in the hotel since then, out of work, leaning on Alex, and burning through my savings. The good news is I've found a share with three other girls, and I'll be moving in there in a week or two if I can land a job."

"You'd better write that address down for us. And the phone number, if they have a phone." Dot handed her a notepad.

Lisa wrote it all down in a slow, childlike hand. The address was way out in Inglewood.

"Now what?" she asked.

"Now we go to work," replied Dot. "Call us in a couple of days and we'll give you an update. I'm assuming it's better if we don't call the hotel."

She got up and shook our hands weakly. She arranged her hat on her head and pinned it in place, pulled on her gloves, and picked up her bag. Dot showed her out and watched as she once again flagged down a cab.

I looked at the clock. It was close to 4:00 p.m.

"Now we go to work?" I said skeptically.

"Now we go to the bar," replied Dot. "Monday we go to work."

Chapter Five

When I arrived at the office on Monday morning, Dot was waiting with coffee for both of us. Suitably fortified, we took two streetcars and a brisk walk over to the Hall of Records. I kept watch for the man in the pinstripe suit, but if he was tailing us, he was doing a good job of it.

The Hall of Records was an unremarkable brick building as dull as its contents. Dot always loved that place, but me, not so much. She has an impressive ability to hyperfocus, while my mind jumps all over the place, so searching the indexes is tough work for me. After a while, the words on the page start to dance around or blur together entirely. I can keep my feet or my mind still, but not both at the same time.

Quickly we—and by 'we' I mean 'mostly Dot'—confirmed some basic facts. In the indexes for 1925, we found a birth registered for a Lisa D'Amico with a Claremont address that matched the one on the envelope Lisa had shown us. The father was identified as Tony D'Amico and the mother as Emma D'Amico. And we found a marriage certificate for Tony and Emma for the same year, just a handful of months before the birth. So far, the story checked out.

After that, we took a ride north to the Hall of Justice, which was where the coroner's office had moved a few years back. We wanted to check out Emma D'Amico's death certificate, and it was too recent to be in the Hall of Records indexes. The Hall of Justice was a beautiful stone building with well-proportioned Greek columns and an impressive entryway with a classical frieze above it. This was a building that told the visitor in no uncertain terms that serious business was conducted here. The city was very proud of it. All we needed now was a justice system to match.

We found the coroner's office tucked away in a back corner on the first floor. Dot suggested that was because it was likely to draw less attention if they could bring the bodies in and out around the back. She had a very logical mind for things like that. An earnest and eager clerk in a pin-striped suit and heavy glasses took us to the reading room and we sat—patiently in Dot's case, fidgeting in mine—while he fetched the appropriate volume of records. He laid it in front of us, reminded us there was no smoking in the reading room, then stepped back while we found the entry and read it:

Date of death: February 12, 1946

Age: 42 years

Cause of death: Barbiturate overdose

Coroner's verdict: Suicide

We looked at each other, both of us stunned.

"Wow," I said. "That was kind of an important detail for Lisa to leave out."

"Seriously. The red flags here are starting to mount up," replied Dot.

"Do we want to ask Lisa about this?" I asked anxiously.

Dot stared into the distance for a minute. I knew better than to interrupt her when she did that. "Not just yet. I feel like there's something very hinky here, and I don't want to scare her off before we know what it is."

I nodded. "None of this is getting us any closer to locating my father, though."

"True enough. We've run the genealogy to ground as much as we can, I think. Going through the last eight years of indexes looking for a death certificate for Tony D'Amico would drive even me to despair. And that's assuming he died in LA. Let's leave that as a last resort. Do you have any other angles?"

"Yeah, actually I do have two. Tax records and draft cards."

"Draft cards I get, assuming he registered. We could also check the voter rolls, although from what you've said about him, I don't hold out much hope he's ever registered there. What's the tax angle?"

I smiled, pleased with myself that I'd beaten Dot to this idea. "There's a property tax on the lot. Somebody must be paying it, or the county would have slapped a lien on it and eventually taken possession."

"Oh, that's good," said Dot. "And if he stopped paying at some point, that might even suggest a year of death to focus our search on. Next stop, City Hall."

We took another streetcar ride back downtown this time. LA would be unlivable without its streetcars, I often thought. It was an odd reflection for somebody who had once made her living driving a cab.

The voter rolls were a bust, which was not a big surprise, so we headed downstairs to the draft office. It was a bland room with three dozen uncomfortable-looking wooden chairs arranged in rows, all of them empty. I tried to imagine it during the war, filled with eager and nervous young men.

At the back of the room was the sort of banged-up wood-topped counter that seems to be found in every government office. Behind it were rows upon rows of drawers, the kind used for index cards. We approached the counter and were greeted by the woman perched on a high chair behind it. If you had called up Central Casting and asked them to send over a meek librarian, this was the woman you would have gotten. Slim and brittle looking, she had mousy brown hair tied back in a bun, and was dressed in a dull gray dress with a frilly white collar and cuffs. Her face hid behind heavy-rimmed spectacles. She looked middle-aged, and probably always had.

"How can I help you?" she asked. We obviously weren't there to register.

"Hi, yes," I replied. "I'm a private investigator working a case, and I'm looking for the draft card of an individual." A lot of people seemed to get very excited about helping a P.I. I guess the movies made them think our work was a lot more dramatic than it really was. This clerk, unfortunately, was not one of them.

"I don't think I can just show you somebody's card. There are confidentiality issues," she said in her timorous little voice.

"What if I told you it was an official investigation?" I said. Technically this wasn't a lie: I didn't actually say it was official, I just asked what might happen if I did say that. I pulled my wallet out of my jacket pocket and let it flop open, showing my P.I. license and my Special Deputy buzzer. Ginnie had leant on a district attorney with the promise of financial support for his re-election to get the police badges for us. Technically, they didn't mean much, but sometimes they impressed people. This was one of those times.

The librarian peered at it for a moment or two. "Well, I suppose I can show you if it's related to a case. Who is it for?"

"His name is Tony D'Amico. Possibly Antony D'Amico, without an 'h'." I spelled the last name out for her.

"And do you know when he was born?"

"Early 1903, but I don't know the exact month."

"OK, then he would have been 37 in 1940. So too old for the first draft. That means we're looking at 1942."

"What happened in '42?" asked Dot.

"They raised the eligible age from 36 to 44. Let me take a look."

She turned to the cabinets, running her finger efficiently over the labels on the front of each drawer until she found the one she wanted. Inside, she quickly located the card we were looking for. She placed it on the counter in front of us. There was his name, his date of birth, and an address in East Los Angeles. Or at least, what his address had been in '42. It was something. Dot flipped the card over and read it out.

"Height, 5'9". Weight, 150 pounds. Hair, black. Eyes, brown. Complexion, olive. Distinguishing marks, two-inch scar above left eyebrow. Sound right?"

"I guess," I replied. "It's kind of a generic description and I was five when I last saw him. I don't remember a scar, but it's been a while. But nothing is obviously wrong." Finally, I felt like we were getting somewhere, although I still wasn't sure it was somewhere I wanted to go.

Dot flipped the card back and copied down the address. We thanked the clerk and made our way downstairs and outside.

"I need lunch," I announced. Dot agreed.

We found a small diner. The lunch rush was long over and we had the place to ourselves, apart from one old geezer sitting up at the counter who looked like he'd been there since before the war. I ordered the spaghetti special and Dot looked at me like I was crazy. She had a big thing about not eating food that might spill or splash on her clothes, and sometimes, I ordered the messiest thing on the menu just to see her reaction. She ordered a grilled tuna sandwich. She would eat it with a knife and fork.

The waitress poured coffee for both of us and shouted our order to the cook in the back. "One radio sandwich and a blue-plate!"

We waited quietly until our food showed up.

"Well, this completely blows up Lisa's plan," said Dot, suddenly breaking the silence.

"What do you mean?" I replied.

"To get her father—your father too, I mean—declared legally dead, he needs to have been missing for seven years. We just proved he was alive and kicking in '42."

"You're right. So much for Plan A. Mind you, that still leaves the possibility of proving he has died since then. Are we obliged to do that for Lisa?"

"The way the contract is written, with no payment up front, we don't have to do anything. We can go back to her at any time with what we've found, and call a halt. No payment, no contract."

"Did you deliberately set it up like that?" I asked, wide-eyed. Dot's cleverness once again amazed me.

She smiled. "Yes. I wanted you to have an out if it got too

much for you. So really, it's up to you. How would you feel about finding proof he's dead? Or about finding him alive for that matter?"

"To be frank, I'm kind of mixed up right now. I hadn't really thought we'd find him at all. I expected we'd do our due diligence, find no trace of him alive, write up a report for Lisa to take to a judge, and that would be the end of it. Knowing he's dead would be one thing. I definitely haven't thought about how I'd feel about him being alive."

"If it were just me, I'd be reluctant to drop the loose end, but he's your father and I don't want to tug on it if you're uncomfortable. Do you want to press on?"

"No. Yes. Maybe," I said, then filled my mouth with a meatball before I said anything even more stupid.

I chewed for a while and thought it over.

"I keep going back and forth on this," I said. "If he's alive, I don't know what he'll be like. My grandma said he was a bum, and it would be kind of disappointing if that turns out to be true. On the other hand, he could have changed, but then I might be frustrated by what I missed out on. Either way, I think I want to know. If we don't continue, I'll always wonder 'what if?' My mom might want to know what became of him too. Especially if he's dead."

Dot looked at me for a few seconds before speaking. "Okay, how about this? After lunch, you chase down your idea about the tax records. Maybe there is something there, like a more recent address. And if that comes up empty, we can at least check out the address we already have after that. But if that all comes up cold, perhaps we've gone as far as we reasonably can. Unless we get really lucky, it could take a lot more work to prove him dead."

"That sounds fair. But what are you doing this afternoon?"

"I have to go and follow a couple of domestic servants to figure out which one is too rich for her own good. Let's meet at Jack's around 6:30."

I noted to myself that when Dot said "around 6:30", she meant she'd be there no later than 6:25. We finished lunch and went our separate ways, Dot heading downtown and me heading back to City Hall to fill my head with paper searches and empty it of thoughts of my childhood.

Chapter Six

I got to the bar around 5:30 p.m. and started on a beer and a Lucky Strike while I was waiting. After a few minutes, some of the cabbies from Red Star drifted in and I joined them to catch up. There were slow days in the office when I missed the driving and especially the camaraderie, but I'd known for a long time that sooner or later, they were going to give my drive to a returning veteran. I felt lucky I'd gotten out ahead of the awkwardness of them letting me go.

Dot arrived five minutes before 6:30 p.m., which I call "early" and she calls "on time." She picked up her straight rye and came over to say hi to the drivers, and then took me away to a high top to talk shop.

She lit up a Kool and took a long draw. "One of our domestics is eating at Romanoff's in Beverly Hills tonight, so either she has a rich and famous boyfriend or she has another source of income," she said. "I'm going to stay on her a couple more days just to be sure, but I think this is going to be a quick wrap."

"Romanoff's is the place run by the fake Russian prince, right?" I asked.

"That's the one. Also known as Harry Gerguson from Brooklyn. Or maybe Hershel Geguzin from eastern Europe, who knows."

"Lot of fake names going around this week," I said. "Must be the time of year."

"There certainly are. Anyway, how did you get on with the tax records?"

"Good. I found two things, one surprising and one not.

It's no surprise that Tony D'Amico hasn't been paying the property tax. But you'll never guess who has."

"You're right, I won't." Dot loved facts and hated guessing games.

"Mammoth Pictures. The property is next door to their backlot, it turns out. What do you figure?"

Dot did her thousand yard stare while her cigarette burned down. Then she came back.

"Okay, try this. Mammoth wants the lot, but if the taxes go unpaid, the city would put a lien on the property, and eventually take ownership. Then they'd auction it off, and let's suppose Mammoth doesn't want to get into a bidding war with whoever is on the other side of the lot."

"Twentieth Century," I said. "I looked it up once I saw Mammoth's name."

"Big money studio. So Mammoth wants a chance to buy it privately if the owner ever turns up, and in the meantime, the city doesn't care who pays the taxes. It might not work out for them, but it's better than risking an auction."

"Now what?" I asked.

"Like we said, we do have an old address for your father. Are you still up for checking it out in the morning?"

"Sure. You know you don't have to come, though."

"Right," said Dot. "Like I'm going to let you do this alone." Again the Big Sister, and again I didn't mind.

We agreed to meet at nine at the office, and we rejoined the cabbies for more drinks.

Chapter Seven

Tuesday morning, I got to the office at the stroke of nine, which of course meant that Dot had made coffee and had been waiting for five minutes already. We fueled ourselves with a cup of joe and set out for East Los Angeles. The rush hour was already over and the near-empty streetcar rattled along noisily. Dot sat in silence; I preferred to straphang for all but the longest of journeys, even when there were plenty of seats. I always liked to properly feel the sway of the streetcar in my body, the chatter of the wheels in my feet, and the swing of the turns. Dot had once suggested that I also liked to be standing in case I needed to run. I hated it when she psychoanalyzed me. Especially when I suspected she was right.

Neither of us said anything for the whole trip. I was wrapped up in my own anxious thoughts, imagining how the scene might play out, and Dot was just naturally quiet, never feeling the need to speak unless she had something worthwhile to say. She had asked me earlier if I knew what I was planning to say. I had said no, and that was enough of an answer for her.

The address was in a neighborhood that could generously be described as 'mixed fortunes'. From the streetcar stop, we walked along a street of unostentatious ranch houses with nicely-kept gardens and well-painted windows and doors, then turned into one lined with side-by-side duplexes, each with a little patch of grass out front that might optimistically be called a front yard. Here the paint was cheaper and more faded, but looked mostly okay. People were still doing their best to keep up appearances.

After two blocks of that, we came to my father's block—or perhaps former block. We would soon find out which one it was. This one was made up of rowhouses in varying degrees of decay. They fronted right up to the sidewalk, each with two steps up to the front door. Some had rusting iron railings on the steps, but most had lost their railings long ago, leaving only rust-red stubs set into the concrete. Some also had boarded up windows scrawled with graffiti. One was a burnt-out-shell, its roof collapsed. It seemed like a miracle the fire hadn't spread to its neighbors. Even the best of them had peeling paintwork or the odd broken window pane patched with wood or cardboard. The few cars parked here were beaters, old and rusted and dented with bald tires. Dot could probably have told me the make and model and year of each—it was kind of her party trick—but it really didn't matter what they had been when new. All of them were probably worth more now as scrap than as cars.

At the end of the street was a small red brick apartment building, four floors high, separated from the row houses by an alley. Junk was scattered in the alley, and at its far end, there was a small wooden hut. I suspected somebody might even be living in it. The brick had once been painted white, and the color still survived in patches. The front and the side that we could see were both tagged with graffiti. The windows were dirty and the place obviously hadn't been repainted in some years. This was my father's last known address.

We went inside and passed a couple of bags of garbage

waiting to go out. The floor, the walls, the stairs, the lightbulbs: everything was dirty. We climbed two flights to where we found my father's apartment. The door was no more battered than the ones on either side.

Dot put her hand on my elbow. She didn't like physical contact much, so for her, this was a rare gesture. "Are you still okay with this? It's not too late to back out," she said, concern obvious in her voice.

"We're here, so let's do it," I replied. "Who knows, he might not be home, or even live here anymore." I stepped up to the door and rapped out a rapid tattoo, then took a half step back. We waited a couple of minutes, me tapping my toes impatiently, Dot enviably calm.

Nothing happened. "One more try?" I said, and Dot nodded. I knocked again. Still no sound from inside.

At that moment, the door to the apartment on the left opened and a middle-aged woman stepped out. She wore a cheap, thin housedress with a frayed hem, nylons with holes and runs, and threadbare slippers. Her hair was wrapped in an equally threadbare towel. She looked us over. Dot was obviously overdressed for this building. I thought I didn't look too out of place in my gabardine pants, plain white blouse, and flight jacket, but it was the kind of neighborhood where it was obvious who did or didn't belong. Her gray face had heavy creases around the eyes and cheeks that cratered dramatically as she drew on her cigarette. The thought of looking like that in 20 years almost made me want to quit smoking. Realistically, she could have been anywhere between 30 and 60 years old. Poverty will do that to a person. That and a lifetime of worries.

She took her cigarette out of her mouth just long enough to speak a few words. "He sleeps late," she told us.

"Tony D'Amico?" I asked.

"That's him. He goes out drinking, comes home late and noisy, and then sleeps it off."

At least we were in the right place. I tried one final knock. She stood and watched. I guessed we were what passed for entertainment around there.

I jumped a little as the door opened. An unshaven, grimy-looking man in baggy, faded jeans and a dirty vest stood there with a half-empty beer bottle in his hand. His hair looked like he had slept in it. The acrid smell of sweat, stale beer and body odor slowly drifted across the threshold.

"What the hell do you want?" he said. Somehow, he managed to do this with his cigarette still in his mouth, stuck to his bottom lip.

I looked him over. He was more or less the most disappointing version of the description on his draft card you could imagine. Skinnier, dirtier, and there was the scar. His clothes hung loose on his frame.

"Tony D'Amico?" I asked him, just to be sure.

"Who's askin'?" he replied, a surly curl to his upper lip.

"Your daughter Joy," I said. I'd planned to break it to him more gently than that, but with his attitude I decided forget it, and jumped right in.

He stared at me long enough to take his cigarette out of his mouth and jab it towards Dot. "Who's that?"

"My friend," I replied. I was in no mood to give up more than that.

"I guess you'd better come in," he said. He turned and

disappeared inside, not waiting to see if we were following him. I looked at Dot, and she nodded. It didn't seem like a great situation, but we'd come all this way out here, and who knew if we'd get another chance to talk to him? Dot left the door open behind her, which seemed sensibly cautious.

The apartment door led into a single room that served as living room, bedroom, and kitchenette. One door led to what I at first assumed was a bathroom. On second thought, it was probably a closet, and there was a shared bathroom down the hall. In a place this old and this cheap, that arrangement seemed more likely than toilets in every apartment. The room matched its owner. The wallpaper was faded and peeling in places. The walls were bare of pictures, although a couple of less-faded rectangles indicated where pictures might have once hung, before they'd been pawned or sold for beer money. On the wall above the window was a green-black patch of mold.

In one corner was a space that could just about qualify to be called a kitchenette. A few dishes were stacked in the small rust-stained sink and appeared to be growing a separate species of mold all their own. Empty beer bottles in a variety of shades of green and brown were strewn around the floor. If they had deposits on them, he could probably make enough money for another half-dozen bottles.

The furniture, if you could call it that, was comprised of a sunken red velour sofa, the cushions pressed flat and the covers worn thin by decades of butts, and an oversize chair that might have been dragged off the street from one block over, left out by somebody hoping the garbagemen might take pity and haul it away. I would like to have watched the process of getting it up the narrow stairs here. Under the window sat a small table, just big enough for one person to sit down and eat dinner, cluttered with a dirty plate and more beer bottles. A sagging cot was pushed up against the opposite wall. There were no curtains in the window, but anybody would have done well to see through the grime on them anyway. It was a mystery to me how the owner of this room had managed to so thoroughly charm Lisa's mother that she had waited for his return. Or for that matter, had once charmed my mother. My head was a churning ocean of anger and disappointment.

My father took the chair, Dot and I the sofa, although Dot looked as though she was trying to have as little contact with the cushion as was physically possible. Tony lit another cigarette from the butt of the previous one and took a slug of beer.

"So you're little baby Joy, all grown up and a long way from home," he said, his voice icy with sarcasm.

I glanced at Dot, who I suspected was feeling protective towards me and homicidal toward him. I tried not to be rattled or rude. "I guess so," I said, as calmly as I could manage.

"Well, I hope you're not here for a handout," he said, gesturing with his free hand to the litter-strewn room.

"No, but I do have some news for you. Emma is dead, in case you still care." I had no desire to break anything gently to this man. I just wanted to get that part of the conversation out of the way, so I could get out of there quickly, and never see him again.

He took another pull of beer, furrowing his brow for a

moment. I briefly thought he might have been trying to remember who Emma was. I wondered just how drunk he was.

"That's a shame," he said without sounding like he meant it. "She must have been only, what, 40-something?"

"Something like that. It was suicide." He hadn't bothered to ask, but at this point, I wanted to twist the knife until I got some sort of reaction from him.

"Huh. She always had that in her," he said flatly.

I don't think I've ever hated somebody so much and so quickly.

"I also know about Lisa," I said. "Any other half-sisters out there I should have heard of?"

He ignored the question, instead taking another pull of beer. I was ready to leave, but Dot wanted to tug on one more thread. "Is it true about you owning the deed to a lot in Century City?" she asked.

He looked over at her as if he had forgotten she was still there. "Yeah, I left it with Emma. She was supposed to sell it to help with the bills. That was about all I could do for her."

"She still had it when she died," I said.

"Huh. I guess I'd like it back then."

I'd had enough. I nudged Dot and announced we had to leave.

"Sure, thanks for visiting your old man," he said.

"Yeah, it's been great. Let's do it again real soon," I replied.

He obviously wasn't going to get up, so we showed ourselves out.

Out on the street, both Dot and I took several deep

breaths to settle ourselves and clear the smell of his room from our noses.

"Wow, your father is a real piece of work, if you don't mind me saying so," said Dot.

"My ex-father," I replied.

"I don't think that's a thing."

"It is now."

Chapter Eight

We were silent all the way back to the office. Lisa called about noon to check in, and I asked her to come and see us that afternoon if she could. We were planning to put away this whole unsatisfactory business as quickly as possible and get back to proper paid work. Dot went out for lunch to watch one of the errant domestic staff, and came back around two looking pleased with herself. She had nailed the staffer eating oysters at lunch.

"Ironically," said Dot, "oysters used to be working class food, and there were tons of them everywhere. New York paved streets with their shells. But then the government made them clean up the business, and suddenly, they were too expensive for working folks. And for some people, expensive means they must be good."

"Nice work," I said. "It's just a shame we'll only get paid for a couple of days."

"Yes, for a couple of hours' work. It makes up a bit for the fact that the Lisa business didn't make you rich."

I smiled weakly. I was trying not to get worked up about missing out on the inheritance. I assumed that once my father got his hands on the deed, he would promptly sell it and then drink the money away. I told myself that I'd only lost something that two days ago I didn't even know existed.

Around 2:15, the bell on the door rang. I got up and peered into the outer office just in time to see a cab pulling away and Lisa coming into the waiting room. She was wearing the same yellow dress we'd seen her in the first time she visited. If she was trying to signal poverty, it was a good move. I waved her through and settled her in one of the chairs in front of my desk where she arranged her hat, bag, and gloves as ritually as she had before. Dot brought her coffee and sat down alongside her. We'd agreed that I would do most of the talking. It might come better from me, since I had a stake in this too. At least in theory.

I briefed Lisa on our father's crummy living situation and bad attitude, and she nodded along. She didn't seem too surprised or too disappointed. But the next thing I said did make her sit up and take notice.

"He said he wants the deed back. Apparently, your mother was supposed to sell the property to help cover expenses, but since she didn't, he wants it returned," I said.

Lisa puckered her lips in thought. "I guess she never lost faith he was coming back. Although we could certainly have used the money. By the way, I brought it like you asked."

She pulled it from her bag and Dot looked it over, then handed it back.

"Emma couldn't have sold it anyway," said Dot. "It's still in his name."

"But he gave it to her," said Lisa.

Dot shook her head. "It doesn't work like that with real estate. You can't simply hand over the deed; the title has to be formally transferred. Mind you, it's not complicated if there's no money changing hands. The owner just fills out a quitclaim form and signs it, and then somebody takes it to City Hall to get the change of ownership registered. But even if he'd done that, it would be his again now. When she died, he was her next of kin. He's in line ahead of you, remember? This just cuts out the need for probate to put it back in his name."

"Does probate take long? Not that it makes any difference now," Lisa asked.

"It depends how backed up they are and how complicated the estate is, especially without a will. It could easily be months."

Lisa looked thoughtful for a few moments, digesting all of that information, then recomposed herself. "Could you give me his address?" she asked. "I think I might want to write to him eventually."

"Okay," I replied, "if you think that's a good idea. But don't expect too much." I wrote it down for her on a notepad, tore off the page and handed it over to her. "I don't recommend visiting, at least not alone. It's not a good neighborhood."

She acknowledged that with a nod. "Thank you both for your efforts, even if it ended in disappointment."

I wasn't sure if her disappointment was learning about our father's poor circumstances, or not getting ownership of the deed, but I had my suspicions.

"What will you do about the money you owe?" I asked. If she was going to hit us up for a 'loan', now would be when it happened. She surprised me.

"I suppose I'll have to sell some of the jewelry my steady gave me. Or pawn the cufflinks he never wears and hope he doesn't notice. Either way, it's not your problem any longer."

If she thought that was going to prompt us to bail her out, she would be disappointed. We all sat in silence for a few moments. Then she got up, limply shook each of us by the hand in turn, gathered her belongings, said her goodbyes, and walked out. The bell rang and the door closed itself behind her. Case closed.

Dot poured both of us coffee and we lit cigarettes.

"I see she's still not interested in building a relationship with her long-lost half-sister," I said. "Do you think she might come back, pleading desperation to pay off her imaginary bookie?"

"Perhaps. Something's still off," said Dot, "and it's making my brain itch."

"I'll tell you what seems cockeyed to me," I replied. "My father didn't mention Lisa at all. Didn't ask after her, or wonder how I knew her, or anything, not even after I mentioned her mother's death."

Dot put her cup down and sat up straight. "You're right. I'll tell you something else that doesn't sit right," she said. "Lisa didn't bring it up either. In her place, wouldn't you have wanted to know whether your father had asked after you?"

"Yeah, that might be even more off, however little she cared about him. But I guess we're just going to have to live with that mystery."

"I hate mysteries," said Dot miserably, and drained her coffee. I could see I was going to have to take her to Jack's later to buy her a drink.

Chapter Nine

It was Thursday at exactly 9:15 a.m. when the phone rang. We were both still hugging our first cup of coffee, and neither one of us wanted to answer. After four rings, I accepted defeat and picked up.

It was Lisa. "Joy? Is that you?" she blurted out. She sounded breathless. I signaled Dot to pick up her own extension and listen in.

"Listen, I'm over by my father's apartment, and I think something's wrong!" she said rapidly.

"Okay, slow down. Take a breath," I replied. "Now, where exactly are you?"

"I'm in a drug store a block over from his building. Hold on." I heard some muffled back-and-forth, presumably Lisa talking to somebody else. She came back on. She named an intersection and Dot jotted the address down. "I heard loud noises from inside his apartment. I think he's had some kind of fall. Can you come here quickly?"

"Okay," I said. "Stay calm. Have a cup of coffee and a cigarette and wait for us at the drugstore. We'll be there in 20 minutes."

"Alright," she said and hung up.

Dot looked across at me. "Twenty minutes?" she said. It had taken us the better part of 40 the previous day.

"It sounded urgent," I said. I picked up the phone again and dialed Madge at the Red Star taxi garage. She was as efficient as always, took down my request for a cab, and hung up.

We gathered our purses and went outside to wait. The cab

pulled up about five minutes later and we scooted into the back seat. I desperately wanted to be up front driving, but I tamped down the urge. Surprisingly, I didn't recognize the driver. He must have been new since my days at Red Star.

We hit some traffic crossing town and got there in 25 minutes. I went to pay the driver, but he waved me off. "Madge told me it goes on your account," he said. That was her way of saying it was free, and I tipped the driver a buck.

Inside the drugstore, Lisa was sitting up at the counter. She was wearing her other cheap dress, the floral print one. Judging by the ashtray in front of her, she'd had more than one cigarette while she was waiting. She stubbed out the one she was smoking, dropped some change on the counter for her coffee, and shuffled off the stool.

It took us just a few minutes to walk over to the apartment building, and soon we were standing outside the door to my father's apartment again. It was locked.

"We need to call the police!" urged Lisa.

"I've got this," said Dot, calmly. She pulled her lockpicks from her bag, and had the door unlocked in a matter of seconds.

I opened the door carefully, peeked inside, then opened it fully and stepped in. Dot and Lisa followed right behind me. The room looked much the way it had when Dot and I had been there the day before. I took in the same worn furniture, the same grubby windows, and the same scattered trash. An empty bottle of bourbon stood by the sink. The only other change was Tony D'Amico's body, suspended by the neck from the closet door.

We all stopped and stared for a couple of seconds.

Dot broke the silence. "I don't know if he's still alive, but we have to get him down."

He was hanging by a narrow leather belt that had been buckled around his neck, the loose end slipped between the closet door and the frame. His feet were just a few inches from the floor. A couple of feet away, a kitchen chair lay on its side. It looked like he had stood on the chair, then kicked it away. I tried to pull the door open, but it stuck fast.

Dot went over to the kitchenette and in the drawer, found the one sharp knife. I set the chair upright, climbed up on it, and started to saw at the belt. I got no more than half way before the belt tore through and the body tumbled loudly to the ground. I stepped down, knelt down beside him, unbuckled the belt from around his neck, and tried to find a pulse. There was nothing in his wrist and nothing in his neck. I put my face close to his mouth, but could not feel any breath. I stood up.

"He's gone," I said.

Lisa sat down heavily on the sofa. "What now?"

"I'll go back to the drugstore and call the police. Don't touch anything while I'm gone. It tends to upset the police," said Dot.

Lisa was still as a rock, staring at the body. I put two Lucky Strikes in my mouth, lit them both, and put one of them between Lisa's lips. She took a pull then let out a long breath. I examined myself for any kind of emotional reaction and found none.

A tap on the door made me look up. The lady from next door was standing in the doorway, wearing the same housedress from yesterday, and taking in the scene with apparent indifference. I guessed she had been curious about the noise. She took her own cigarette from her mouth.

"Coffee?" she asked.

"Yeah, that would be helpful," I replied. She disappeared back into her own apartment. Lisa and I sat silently. The woman reappeared a couple of minutes later, a mug in each hand. The mugs were chipped and dirty and the coffee smelled weak, but we didn't care. She stayed in the room, standing just to the side of the doorway. This was probably the most interesting thing that had happened in the building in a long while.

After about ten minutes, Dot returned. She declined the offer of coffee and took the chair that my father had been sitting in alive, 48 hours earlier. More minutes passed in silence.

Eventually, we were interrupted by a knock on the open door. A hispanic man in a smart brown pinstripe suit, white shirt and dark tie was standing in the door, holding open his wallet to display his police buzzer.

"Detective Ramirez, Los Angeles PD. Homicide," he announced. He looked young for a detective, maybe my age. I guessed he might be the most junior detective in the squad, and therefore, assigned to deal with this probably-not-a-homicide scene. He walked over and crouched by the body, and then went through the same routine I had to verify he was dead. He poked the cut-off belt with his toe.

"He hung himself?" he asked.

"'Hanged'" said Dot.

I glared at her. Sometimes she just can't help herself.

Ramirez ignored her. "How are you all feeling?" he asked.

"We've seen worse," said Dot. It was true. The last corpse we'd stumbled over had been dead for a day. That was a whole lot more unpleasant. Ramirez looked at us with surprise and, I hoped, a little more respect. Lisa just nodded. I had no idea what that was supposed to mean.

Ramirez made a brief tour of the rest of the room. He pulled on a thin cotton glove and opened the closet door, touching as little of the handle as possible, and picked up the other half of the belt from the floor. There was a knot tied in the end of it. That was what had kept the belt from slipping down. It was also what had stopped me from opening the door.

"What's been touched?" he asked.

I raised my hand like we were in class. "I cut him down. I had to stand that chair up to do it. When we came in, it was sideways on the floor over there." I pointed. "And I checked the pulse, same way you did. That's it." He nodded.

"No rigor mortis, so death was recent," he said, as much to himself as to us. "So who wants to tell me a story?" He pulled out a notebook and a pen.

"You should probably start," I said to Lisa. "Since you were here first."

"Um, okay," she said, a little nervously. "I'm Lisa D'Amico. I got here this morning sometime after nine I guess, and I knocked on the door. There was no answer, and then I heard a loud clattering noise. I knocked a couple more times, and then I got worried, so I went and found a phone and called Joy."

"Which one of you is Joy?" he asked.

I raised my hand again. "It was 9:15 precisely when she rang."

"How sure are you about that?" asked Ramirez.

"Very," said Dot. "We meticulously log all our calls, incoming and outgoing."

"Who are you?" he asked.

"I'm Dot Stone. I'm Joy's partner."

"Her what now?"

"Oh, right. We're private detectives, we're working a case on behalf of Lisa." She pulled her wallet with her license from her bag and I did the same.

Ramirez was suitably unimpressed by our Special Deputy buzzers, but he noted down our license details. "Rookies, huh?" he said, writing down the dates our licenses had been issued. He had the look of a man who had just realized that a simple suicide write up was turning into a paperwork nightmare. "Can you tell me what the case is about?"

I looked at Lisa for permission and she nodded her assent.

"Was," I replied. "We were helping Lisa trace her father who she hasn't seen for eight years."

"And that's him, I take it," said Ramirez, pointing his pen at the corpse. "Nice detective work."

I scowled at his sarcasm, then let it go. "Dot and I tracked him down and came here two days ago - Tuesday - to verify he was still at this address. We talked for a little while and then we left."

"How did he seem? Suicidal?"

"He seemed fairly miserable, but look around. Who wouldn't be? And he wasn't pleased to see me. But nothing suggested this. Oh, I should mention, he's also my father.

Lisa and I are half-sisters."

Ramirez now had the look of a man who could sense a migraine coming on. "Were you looking for him too?"

"Only professionally. He left when I was very young, and I've never really cared to chase him. What little I learned about him yesterday was enough to know I hadn't missed anything. Anyway, we reported back to Lisa what we'd found, and that seemed like 'case closed,' as far as we were concerned."

He turned to Lisa. "So then you came here looking for him?"

"Yes," she replied. "I was hoping that maybe we could be reconciled."

Ramirez flipped back through his notes a couple of pages. "Okay, that brings us back to 9:15. You get the call." The last part was addressed to me.

"Lisa seemed very upset, so we high-tailed it over here in a taxi. We picked up Lisa from the drugstore a couple of blocks away, and walked back here. We knocked on the door a few times and when we didn't get a reply, we… uh…" I paused.

Dot apparently decided an ugly truth was better than a beautiful lie. "I picked the lock," she said.

Ramirez kneaded his temple. "I'm going to write down that the door was unlocked, which is technically true. Don't make me regret it. What next?"

"Well, the rest you know," I said. "We found the body, I cut it down, and Lisa and I waited here while Dot went to call the police."

He turned to the neighbor. "What about you?"

"I'm just the neighbor," she said.

"See or hear anything?"

"I heard her knocking," she said pointing her cigarette at Lisa, "and later a thump. I guess that was the body coming down."

"What about the neighbor the other side, think he might know anything?"

"He's stone deaf. And he only opens his door to buy beer and bread."

"Uh huh." We waited while Ramirez caught up with his notes. Then he went back over to the body, knelt beside it, and started to go through the pockets. When he stood back up, he was holding a couple of sheets of paper. He unfolded them and looked them both over.

"What's that?" Dot asked.

Ramirez held the first sheet out to her. "Look, don't touch," he said. Dot clasped her hands behind her back and read it out for us.

"I have been a lousy father and a lousy husband. I'm sorry, but it's too late for me to fix that. I have been out of my families' lives for too long and now I am getting out of them for good. I don't have anything to leave you except some land that was promised to Emma, so now it belongs to Lisa."

"It's handwritten and signed," Dot added. "It's not dated, but I think we can infer that part." Turning to Ramirez, she explained, "Emma was Lisa's mother, but she and Tony were long separated. She died some months ago."

He jotted that down. "Let me show you what else he had," he said.

He held up the other sheet. "It's a quitclaim for a piece of land over in Century City, signed over to Lisa D'Amico. Is this the land the note mentioned?"

Detective Ramirez clearly did not like making assumptions, however compelling they might seem. I admired his thoroughness. Dot and I looked across at Lisa, unsure how much she wanted to reveal. She spoke up.

"My father gave the deed to my mother just before he left us. She was supposed to sell it if she needed money, but she never did. I guess he never signed it over to her properly." That seemed like enough, and neither Dot nor I added any more detail.

Ramirez sighed heavily. "Okay, I think we're done here. I just need full names and addresses, and phone numbers if you have them. And I need you three to come to the station, this afternoon if possible, and sign your statements. I'll have the coroner come over and clean up here." He handed us all business cards.

"What about the quitclaim?" said Lisa.

"It's evidence for now. You'll get it back in a few days," he replied.

Lisa looked for a moment like she was going to protest, but let it go.

We walked back to the drugstore and I called Madge for another taxi. I felt a little guilty taking advantage of her again, but I didn't want to drag Lisa on and off streetcars. She seemed okay for the moment, but shock can be delayed and can come on suddenly. I knew the driver this time so I rode up front where I'm comfortable, and Dot sat with Lisa in the back. After a couple of blocks, I caught sight of a bright red Hudson in our side mirror, a half-block or so back. It was two cars back when we pulled up at the next light. We dropped Lisa off at the Belvedere, and I tried not to stare as the Hudson cruised past. The driver could easily have been the same skinny guy from the Belvedere's lobby.

We took the cab over to Jack's bar. A neon sign in the window claimed it was open all hours, and I had yet to find reason to doubt that. The clock on the wall said that it was only a few minutes after 11:00 am. The early morning drunks had gone home, or wherever else they went when they weren't here, and the lunchtime drinkers hadn't started yet, so we had the place to ourselves. We settled in at a high top with drinks and cigarettes. It was a routine that always made me more comfortable. I felt a little guilty not inviting Lisa to join us, but I barely knew her and didn't particularly want to. I sipped at my bourbon and Dot took a slug of her rye, spotting the glass down on the beer mat she insisted on using despite the state of the tables.

"Drinking at Jack's in the morning is officially our post-corpse tradition," joked Dot.

"We've only ever seen two corpses," I pointed out. She seemed to be handling this one a lot better than the first one. I hoped I was.

"Once is a precedent, twice is a tradition."

"Okay then." We clinked glasses.

"How are you feeling?" asked Dot.

"About the suicide of the father I hadn't seen in 20 years, then saw two days ago for just long enough to discover what a jerk he is? I'm not exactly broken up. Honestly, I'm not sure I'm feeling anything. It's kind of an emotional shrug."

"Makes sense."

"I hope Lisa is doing as well as she's pretending," I said, switching tracks. "Both parents committing suicide in the space of six months, that's got to be rough."

"To lose one parent may be regarded as a misfortune, but to lose both looks like carelessness," said Dot.

"What?"

"It's a quote. Oscar Wilde. Never mind. Look, what I'm saying is, two suicides seem like too much of a coincidence to me, especially with all the other questionable circumstances around this business."

"Yeah, it definitely seems hokey. What do you want to do about it, though? We don't have a case anymore. Not even one we're working for free."

"I want to talk to Detective Ramirez. Maybe he can be persuaded to investigate this as more than just a simple suicide. But first, I want to get some lunch. Rye on an empty stomach is getting to me."

Chapter Ten

It was another boringly perfect LA afternoon, and even the regular rain clouds were too embarrassed to ruin it. We took the Red Line across town to the address on Ramirez's card. I didn't want to take too much advantage of Madge's generosity, and I knew she wouldn't ever let me pay for a cab. We'd called ahead to make sure Ramirez would be in, and by 2:30, we were sitting across his desk from him.

The squad room was a large open space with three dozen cheap-looking desks arranged in a four by nine grid that reminded me of a typing pool, albeit a very noisy and untidy one. Homicide shared the room with Vice and a couple of other smaller squads, Ramirez told us. Maybe one third of the desks were occupied. All of them were messy in a way that was probably making Dot itch all over, except Ramirez's. His was completely clear, apart from an inbox to his left, an outbox to his right, and a blotter pad centered perfectly between them.

At the far end of the room were three glassed-in offices that Ramirez told us were for the Captain, the duty Lieutenant, and any lead detective who happened to be in. This one was a 'Detective-three,' Ramirez explained. Ramirez himself was a 'Detective-one'. One long wall was made up entirely of windows, but they didn't let in much light. The low police building was overshadowed by City Hall right next door. On the other long wall were a row of rooms with frosted glass. Ramirez explained they were interview or conference rooms. Apparently, there were secure interrogation rooms on the floor above with one-way mirrors for watching the action.

He handed each of us a typed-up sheet and we read through them. It was an accurate enough account of what we'd told him, and as promised, he'd left out any mention of Dot's skill with lockpicks. We each signed them and handed them back, and Ramirez tucked them into a manilla folder that he dropped in his top drawer. He looked at us for a long second, leaning back in his chair.

"Would you ladies like some coffee?" he asked.

Dot and I looked at each other, both equally unsure what was going on. I didn't think he was flirting while he was on the clock, but a lot of girls wouldn't have minded if he was. He was dark haired, olive skinned, and had a firm chin with high cheekbones. He was sharply dressed for a cop, and was kind of cute, if that was your type.

"Sure," I said on behalf of both of us. "We both take it black, no sugar."

He shook his head. "The coffee here is dishwater. You ever had proper Mexican coffee? Café de olla?"

"No, but I'll give it a try," I said.

"Okay," said Dot, more tentatively.

Ramirez stood up, slipped into his suit coat, and guided us out of the squad room, through the lobby, and out the front door. We walked three blocks in silence and arrived in front of a small storefront. The sign over the window said Café del Sol. Each letter was striped red, white, and green like the Mexican flag. We stepped inside and a short, stout, very brown-skinned woman with the blackest hair I'd ever seen and wrinkles you could hide quarters in immediately greeted us all in Spanish, then switched to English.

"Hey Eddie," she called out from behind the counter. "The usual?"

"Make it three," he replied.

"Are you sure? Do the Anglos know what they are getting?"

"No, but they are going to love it."

While they were talking, I looked around the place. There were the kind of café tables you saw everywhere these days, plastic topped two and four seaters in bright primary colors, and a chrome-fronted counter with half a dozen stools. A small handful of other customers had scattered themselves around, each sitting alone with a coffee in front of them. Ramirez led us to a four top and we sat ourselves down just as we had in his office, with him on one side and us side by side on the other.

"So, Detective, is this a social meeting or are we still on the record?" asked Dot.

"Call me Eddie, please," he said. "And we are as much off the record as a cop ever is."

"Meaning what?" I asked.

"Meaning if you confess to murdering my suicide victim, I'm still going to book you. But otherwise, I'm officially not taking notes."

"Fair enough. And as long as we're being informal, I'm Joy and she's Dot. So what are we doing here?"

"My Detective-three wants me to put this case away quickly as a suicide and get back to what he called 'real work'. He says our closure rate is too low."

"And you don't want to, I take it?"

We were interrupted just then by the waitress setting three

little clay mugs in front of us. Each one held coffee that was darker than a coal mine. I leaned forward and sniffed. I detected cinnamon, cloves, some sweetness, and something else I couldn't identify.

"Take it slowly," said Eddie. "It's a lot stronger than what Americans call coffee."

I took a sip. It was deep and rich and warmly scented. "I think you just ruined regular coffee for me forever," I said.

"I'm going to need to find more excuses to visit City Hall," said Dot.

"So. How many things about that suicide scene seemed wrong to you?" said Eddie.

"I hardly know where to start," said Dot.

I sat back to watch and enjoy. This kind of thing was Dot's playground.

"Okay, go," said Eddie.

"First, the suicide letter makes no sense. He left the property to Lisa rather than splitting it between both his daughters. Who does that? What makes that even stranger is that he just saw Joy two days ago, and he never even asked after Lisa. Which, by the way, is darn strange in its own right. And I don't believe he got so remorseful about his years of family failings in the last 48 hours that he suddenly decided to end it all."

"Yeah, that all sounds off," said Eddie. "And to half-ass the attempt at reparations like that, too. What do you make of the quitclaim?"

"Two days ago, he had no idea that he couldn't just hand over the deed to somebody. And then apparently, after our visit, he went over to City Hall, got the proper form, brought it home, filled it out, and folded it neatly with the suicide note. Does that seem likely?"

"No. Something else was off about the note and the quitclaim. The signatures looked close to identical. Nobody signs their name the exact same way twice, least of all a suicidally desperate alcoholic."

"Good point. You're thinking the signatures were forged?"

"They could easily be, and probably were both traced from one original. Amateur mistake. And I wish I had a writing sample for my handwriting guy to compare the note with."

"Lisa has some envelopes he sent to her mother," I said.

"Any chance I could see them?" asked Eddie.

"Zero," I offered. "When Lisa shows up again, it will be to sign her statement and get the quitclaim back. She might promise to bring in the envelopes, but once she has that deed, she'll be halfway to 'Frisco before you can blink. I guarantee it."

"Another thing," said Dot. "Where did the pen he wrote the note with go? There was no pen on the table, and nowhere to put one away. There was only the cutlery drawer, but it wasn't in there when I fetched the knife. That note was not written in that room."

"Wow, you two have got a real Sherlock and Mycroft thing going here," I said. Dot glared at me. She really did not like Sherlock Holmes stories, and it was guaranteed to needle her if I compared her to him. I should really stop teasing her like that.

"Then there's the empty bourbon bottle," said Dot,

returning to her theme. "Did that apartment look like the home of a bourbon drinker to you?"

"No way. He was strictly a beer guy," said Eddie.

"When I was getting the knife from the drawer, I noticed that the drain stank of bourbon."

"You think somebody poured the bourbon down the drain to make it look like he'd drunk the whole bottle? And they weren't thorough about washing it away?"

"Yes. I think a couple of shots from the bourbon bottle were used to drug him and then someone dumped the rest. If you could get the coroner to do a toxicology report, I bet you'd find barbiturates in his bloodstream."

He tilted his head and looked intrigued. "Goofballs? What makes you think that?"

I chimed in again. "Lisa's mother died a few months back and it was ruled a suicide by barbiturate overdose. But now we're having serious doubts about that one too."

"No chance my Detective-three is going to let me push for an autopsy on this one," said Eddie. "He just wants it closed. But here's another thing that's wrong. Hanging is a very reliable way to kill yourself, but it's also a very nasty one. It takes several minutes, and it's terrifying while it's happening. I don't care how determined to die somebody is, they're going to thrash around until they pass out. But I didn't see any kick marks on the door."

"And the neighbor didn't report hearing anything like that," said Dot. "She only heard Lisa knocking, and then later, the thud of the body hitting the ground when Joy cut him down. And she seemed like the kind of neighbor who sees and hears everything."

"Yes, and the other thing she didn't hear was the chair being kicked away," said Ramirez, nodding. "That should have been noisy enough. Unless it wasn't kicked away, it was just placed on the floor to look like it."

They both paused for thought.

"If you ever want a job with the LAPD, let me know," said Eddie. "I'd love to have you on the squad."

"I'm flattered, but I like being my own boss," smiled Dot.

"Will you two just kiss and get it over with already?" I said.

Eddie laughed and Dot blushed.

"Okay, so it looks very much like we have a murder scene clumsily staged to look like a suicide," he said. "So who is our murderer, and who forged the paperwork?"

"Lisa is the obvious suspect," I replied. I felt like it was time I offered something. "She's the only one with anything to gain from our father's death. And I think she called Dot and me to witness her shocked so-called discovery of the body. She might have worried it would look suspicious if she was the only one to 'find' him dead."

"Makes sense," said Eddie, "but she can't have done it alone. There's no way she could have lifted D'Amico's unconscious body up to put the belt over the door. We're looking for a man, and a strong one at that. Almost certainly two, if you've ever tried moving an unconscious body."

"Or six women with a ladder," Dot said. Eddie and I stared at her. Sometimes I couldn't tell whether Dot was trying to make a joke or just being relentlessly logical. "Never mind," she added.

"Okay, so we're looking for a big guy," I said. "And I can

think of one. The other day, we saw Lisa at the Belvedere hotel in West LA, pretending to be Mrs. Alex Daubman. And Mr. Daubman looked like he was solidly built."

"It's possible I suppose," said Dot, "but it's a bit of a leap from just seeing them together."

"Drugs or poison are usually a woman's murder weapon," I said, thinking again about my true crime magazines. "So maybe we're looking at the two of them in cahoots. But you're right, we really don't have anything else to tie him into this business. There are lots of big guys in Hollywood."

"The name Daubman doesn't mean anything to me," said Eddie, "but I can check it out. I'm going to have to do it on the q.t. though, until I have something solid to show my Lieutenant and my Detective-three."

"We're going to stay on this too," I said, and then realized I shouldn't be taking Dot's agreement for granted. I looked to her for confirmation.

"For sure," she said to me. "I'm not going to leave it like this. You deserve to know."

"I'll call you if I find anything on Daubman," Eddie said.

"We'll do the same," said Dot.

We all got up and Eddie shook our hands. I noticed his shake with Dot lingered a lot longer than mine.

We left Eddie inside the café and walked in silence over to a stop on the Red Line, and waited for a streetcar.

Once we were on board and settled, I turned to Dot. "Geez Louise, kid. You could have given him a little encouragement!"

Dot looked baffled. "What are you talking about?"

"Eddie! He obviously wanted to ask you out. He just

needed a little hint you were interested.”

“Don’t be silly. We were just having a really interesting conversation. You know it’s not often I meet somebody with a mind like mine. Besides, why would he want to ask me out?”

“I dunno, maybe because you’re smart and pretty and the two of you got on like a house on fire?”

“Oh. I honestly didn’t notice.”

“You never do. I’m going to have to start nudging you. Or maybe clubbing you over the head,” I said.

As far as I knew, Dot hadn’t had a date since she’d broken up with Mikey, a cabbie friend I’d set her up with. They had dated for a few weeks and she’d said he was a nice guy and easy to be with, but the only thing they really had in common was a love of dancing. I’d barely known her when I’d introduced them, but I hoped I knew her well enough now to make a better match. Not to mention, I had a feeling she also struggled to shake the feeling of guilt about the beating Mikey had suffered trying to protect her from a mob goon called Moretti. That might have been why she was so reluctant to get back into the pool. That, and the fact that she almost never realized when a guy was making a pass.

“You do think he’s cute, right?” I asked.

“And smart,” replied Dot. “Which, for future reference, is my number one criterion.”

It was close to five by the time we got back to the office. We called it a day.

Chapter Eleven

Friday, we were both out doing legwork on cases that would actually pay the bills. I got back to the office around three, and Dot was already there. She had made a pot of coffee and poured a cup for me as soon as she saw me coming through the door. I sniffed it and thought about yesterday's Mexican coffee. It was hard to believe this stuff came from the same plant, but it would have to do.

The phone rang and I picked up. It was Eddie, and I signaled Dot to pick up her extension.

"You girls need to get an answering service," he said. "I've been trying to reach you for a couple of hours."

"What's the dope, ace?" I asked.

"Lisa is coming here at four to sign her statement and pick up the quitclaim."

"You going to give it to her?" said Dot.

"I don't have a choice. Officially, the case is a suicide and will be closed as soon as I finish the paperwork. I have no excuse to hold onto it."

"Is there any way to block her from getting the deed transferred into her name?" I asked. Everybody was quiet for a moment or two.

"I doubt it," said Eddie. "She'll probably take it right next door to City Hall to get it processed. Next step is presumably to find a buyer and skedaddle."

"Can't she be prosecuted? If the signature was forged, surely that's fraud at the very least," said Dot.

"I guess so, if you can find anybody that cares enough. Homicide certainly doesn't, and I don't know who else here would. As of now, both parents' deaths are tagged as suicide, and an unimportant scrap of land changed hands. So unless you can prove one or both of the deaths was murder, the lieutenant's not even going to take your call. Sorry. I wish I could do better."

"Dammit," I said. "I hate this."

"Me too," said Dot. "But if the police and the DA aren't interested, I don't know where we go from here. I guess we've heard the last of Lisa D'Amico or Daubman or whoever."

"Not quite," said Eddie. "When she comes in, I'm going to put her in an interrogation room and pick at her story a bit to see if I can find a hole in the timeline. Do you two want to listen in?"

"She won't know we're there?" I asked.

"Nope. The rooms are set up to make sure of that."

"We can be there in 30 minutes. Is that soon enough?" said Dot.

"That's perfect."

We were right on time, and Eddie met us in the lobby and took us up to the third floor.

"She's been cooling her heels for about ten minutes," he said. "I find that helps to increase the anxiety. And anxious people make mistakes. When we're done, wait here till I've made sure she's clear of the building. Then I'll fetch you."

He showed us into the darkened back room, put his finger to his lips, and closed the door on us. Dot took one seat in the row of chairs and I stood in front near the window, shifting my weight from foot to foot. We were looking slightly down on the room. There was a single bright overhead light, but everything was dimmed by the one-way mirror. The light hung centrally over a battered wooden table that had large metal loops screwed into it, presumably so violent prisoners could be restrained. Lisa was sitting in an uncomfortable-looking wooden chair and facing us, even though she didn't know it. She looked a lot less calm than she had sitting in our office. Eddie came in and sat down.

"Thanks for coming in today," he said. "This shouldn't take long." He opened the folder he was carrying, pulled out a statement form, and handed it across the table.

"Please go ahead and read this statement, and let me know if you want to change anything."

She squared up the paper on the table, leaned over it, and took her time reading it. Then she straightened up.

"Yes, that's accurate," she said.

"Okay," said Eddie, and he pulled a pen from his pocket. He went to pass it to her, but as she reached out to take it, he pulled it back. She looked confused.

"Because," he continued, "there are a couple of things bothering me about your story."

"Oh," she said, sitting up very straight. "What's the problem?"

"Well, it just seems like a bit of a coincidence that a couple of days after you learn he's alive, your father decides to kill himself and leave his only property of value to you alone, despite not having had any contact with you for years."

She frowned. "Perhaps the visit from Miss Stone and Miss D'Amico kicked up some memories in him, and some regret?" she said.

"I suppose it's possible. Then there's the other

coincidence that you were standing outside his door at the exact moment he kicked over the chair and hanged himself. Coincidences bother me."

I couldn't help noticing he had picked up Dot's correction, and smiled quietly to myself.

"Yes, I suppose that's odd. Unless he was waiting specifically for me to knock, for some reason. Perhaps to have some kind of witness. Perhaps he really wanted to be found before he died, but I was too slow. I understand that a lot of people who attempt suicide don't really intend to succeed. Who knows what is going through the mind of a suicidal man?"

"When your mother overdosed, did she intend to succeed?"

Lisa momentarily raised herself from her seat, then sat back down. She became very stiff. "That was very cruel, Detective," she pouted.

Eddie shrugged. He leant back in his chair and twirled his pen between his fingers for a few seconds, letting her stew. "Are you sure there's nothing you want to change, before I go back to the apartment building and interview the neighbor again?"

The seconds became a minute. Finally, Lisa dropped her head and looked like she might be crying, or was at least trying to. I'd seen that performance one time too many to be fooled. She raised her face again.

"Okay, yes, there is something I left out. I went to see him on Wednesday, the day after I met with Miss Stone and Miss D'Amico. I didn't want to wait any longer to see him."

Eddie pulled a notepad from his folder. "Okay, tell me

what happened."

"I guess it must have been about noon. He let me in and we talked, mostly about how bad things had been for Emma, how she'd never given up hope of him coming back, and how I'd helped her all those years. At the end, he seemed genuinely regretful. He said he wanted to do something for me that he should have done for her when she was alive, and asked me to come back the next morning. I guessed he might have decided to pass the deed on to me, but I never expected… what we found."

Eddie stared at her. "And you didn't mention this earlier. Why?"

"I thought it made me look like I was involved in his killing himself. Setting him up, maybe. I decided to tell a simpler version. And it wasn't exactly a lie. I just left out some things you didn't ask about directly."

"And you're telling me now. Why?"

"Because if you go snooping around his neighbors, one of them will probably say they saw me, and it's going to come out anyway. Better that I own up now."

He stared at her some more, and drummed his fingers on the table.

"If I write it up that way, will you sign to that?"

She nodded.

Eddie stood up, taking back the statement he'd given her, picked up his folder and notepad, and left the room. We waited patiently for 10 minutes for him to come back. This time the statement ran to two pages. She read it through again, signed it, and pushed it across the table to him.

"Can I have my quitclaim now?" she asked.

Eddie pulled it from his folder and handed it across. "I hope that turns out to be worth it to you," he said.

She scowled at him very briefly; it passed so quickly I might have imagined it.

"Come on, I'll walk you out," he said.

We waited again for Eddie to return. Eddie led us downstairs to the lobby where we stood in a small circle.

"What do you think?" he said.

"I think she's a terrible liar," said Dot.

One of Dot's remarkable talents was that tone and body language almost completely passed her by. All she paid attention to was the content of the words, and in this case she had decided that Lisa's story didn't hang together. Socially, that was a bit of a liability, but it made her a fantastic interviewer.

"Either she's telling the truth about a ridiculous series of events, or she's a bold actress and a stone cold killer," I said. "I could go either way."

"In either case, I don't think we'll ever see her again," said Dot.

"Hey, I'm sorry about all this," said Eddie. "It's a thoroughly unsatisfactory outcome, and I wish I could do more. I really like you two and I hope we can see each other again."

"It's okay," said Dot. "We know it's not your fault."

I had a mischievous thought.

"Listen, we all need cheering up. Are you free tonight?"

"I could be. What are you thinking?" said Eddie

"Do you like to dance?" I asked.

"Of course," said Eddie.

"Well, I have a date of my own tonight, but Dot loves to dance."

Dot stared at me wide-eyed and open-mouthed. She clapped her mouth shut again.

"Pick her up at six," I said. "We'll be at our office."

"That's perfect," he replied, grinning like an idiot.

We said our goodbyes and stepped outside.

As we stepped aboard the Red Line car, Dot was still staring at me with some mix of anger, confusion, and gratitude, although I couldn't say in what proportion.

By the time we got back to the office, it looked like she had settled on mostly gratitude, to my relief. She made coffee, we lit cigarettes, and we settled at our desks. I looked across the room at her and risked a question.

"How is it you're so good at analyzing things, but so bad at picking up on other people's emotions?"

She paused for a moment. "I'm not sure I can explain it well to somebody like you. You're so good at emotions," she said. "Frankly, I don't really understand other people who aren't analytical. It's like they can't see the plain facts in front of them, and instead see what they want to be true, or what they feel is right. But for me… emotional reactions are like a code with no key. Give me enough time and enough clues and I can probably figure them out, but in the moment they're happening, I'm lost."

"That must be tough," I said.

"It does cause a lot of misunderstandings. I have a habit of offending people and having no idea what I did. And of course, I usually have no idea when a guy is showing interest until it's way too late."

"So are you okay with me asking Eddie out for you?"

"I am now. He's really interesting. And yes, he's cute. At first, I was worried that it might mess up a really useful contact for us if we break up, but I'm telling myself it'll be fine. After all, Mikey and I are still friends."

"I'm relieved," I said.

"On a related note," said Dot, "when am I going to meet one of your dates?"

That took me by surprise.

"It's… tricky," I said.

Dot said nothing. She was very good at waiting quietly. Most people feel compelled to fill a silence.

I gathered my courage. "All my dates are women," I finally said.

"I thought so," said Dot, a small smile on her lips.

"Why didn't you say something?"

"I was waiting until you were ready."

"How did you figure it out?"

"A few things. One, you never flirt with guys, and I know it's not because you're shy. I've never even seen you look at a guy as if you thought he was attractive, let alone comment that one was cute. And two, you talk a lot about going on dates, but you never talk about the dates afterwards, and especially not about who you're seeing. You've never even told me their names. I've never known a woman who didn't do that with her friends. It was a constant topic when I was in the army, and before that, in college."

"And you're not bothered?"

"For goodness sake, you're not the first lesbian I've known, Joy. I know you think my upbringing was sheltered, but I didn't just grow up in the bookstore. I went to a women's college, and plenty of the girls formed couples. It just wasn't a big deal."

"Yeah, I guess that makes sense." I sighed. "I should have told you a long time ago," I said.

"You should have told me when you were ready, and not a moment sooner," replied Dot.

I got up from my desk, crossed over to hers, and gave her a big hug. But not for too long, because she really doesn't like hugs.

Chapter Twelve

With the paperwork completed and Lisa in the wind, it seemed like we had finally reached the end of the line on an unsatisfactory investigation, for certain this time. We were sure we would never know the truth about Emma's death, nor about Tony's, unless the LA police had a major change of heart. It was all hugely frustrating. I was tempted to go over to the Belvedere to confront her, if she was even still there, but I'd promised Sam no fighting in the lobby. The prospect of him throwing both of us out on the street quickly persuaded me what a bad idea that was.

Life returned to normal for a couple of days. We closed some domestic cases that had been hanging around while we had wasted time on Lisa's wild goose chase, as well as an industrial espionage case, which sounded grander than it was. It was really just an expensive way of saying that the owner of a small machine parts factory suspected his secretary of selling trade secrets. It turned out she was, since she'd handed them off to the secretary of a competitor in the ladies' bathroom at Robinson's on West Seventh Street.

Dot had a second date with Eddie over the weekend. She said he was a very good dancer but refused to be drawn further, only smiling enigmatically.

Monday morning was strictly paperwork until we were interrupted around 11 by the ringing phone. I picked up. It was Sam at the Belvedere. I waved at Dot to pick up too.

"Can you come over and see me? There's something I want to talk about. I'll treat you to lunch at the hotel. The kitchen is surprisingly good here."

"I'll bet it beats our usual cafés," I said.

"Does 11:30 work for you?" he asked.

I looked across at Dot. She nodded.

"Sure. We'll see you then."

"Good. I'll be on my usual spot in the lobby."

We closed up the office and rode a streetcar over to the Belvedere, arriving barely on time, to Dot's obvious discomfort. The skinny guy was sitting in the lobby again. When he saw us walk in, he quickly hid behind his newspaper. I pretended not to notice. Sam was standing over by the front desk, and he walked across to meet us. He moved remarkably gracefully, as men his size rarely do. He shepherded us into the dining room, greeted the host by name, and we were shown to a corner booth and handed menus. I guessed the host assumed that anytime Sam brought guests in, he wanted his conversation to be confidential.

I looked at the prices. They were not outrageous, but certainly way more than we usually paid for lunch. Sam must have caught my expression.

"Don't worry about the tab, this is on me," he said.

"That's very generous of you," said Dot.

"Nah, the hotel picks up the tab when it's for work," he said. "I don't always tell people that when I want to impress them, but I figure you two smart cookies would figure it out anyway."

"Wow, lunch and flattery!" I smiled. "You sure know how to charm."

The waiter took our appetizer orders and Sam ordered a bottle of red wine for the table.

"We don't usually drink at lunch," I said.

"Except when we find a corpse," added Dot.

Sam looked at her sideways, trying to figure out if she was making a joke. I wished him luck, because even I couldn't tell sometimes.

"Does that happen a lot?" he asked.

"Twice, so far," said Dot, precise as always.

The waiter came back with a bottle and presented the label to Sam. He nodded.

The waiter poured glasses for each of us and set the bottle down in the middle of the table. I looked at the label and the jumble of vowels in the name. "Booloo Vineyard?" I asked.

"Beaulieu," said Dot. "It's French."

"Sorry," I replied, "I didn't take French in high school."

Dot glanced at me, probably to see if I was being sarcastic. I liked the fact that she still couldn't always tell either.

"Don't be fooled by the name," said Eddie. "It's a Californian wine and it's pretty good. Some of the vineyards up north are finally starting to come back after Prohibition."

I took a sip and he was right. I could easily see myself finishing a glass and going back for a second one, and I wasn't usually a wine drinker.

"I didn't figure you for a wine guy," I said.

"This'll surprise you, then," he said. "My parents owned a vineyard in Napa. Prohibition ruined them, of course, like most of the other growers. And all America got out of it was that it made the Mob more powerful."

He sounded bitter. He had every right to be.

I could feel Dot getting antsy beside me. She was uncomfortable with these social niceties and desperately wanted to jump into the serious business. Food arrived, and

Dot took the opportunity to change the subject. "This is lovely," she said, "but I'm dying to know what it is that couldn't be discussed over the phone."

"We could've done this on the horn, for sure," replied Sam, "but I like an excuse to eat well. And for good company."

"So what's up?" prompted Dot. I could hear the impatience in her voice.

"First off, thanks for the tip on the Daubman dame," he said. "Believe it or not, she really did try to cash a check."

"Really? You said no, I take it?" I replied.

"For sure. She had a check made out to 'Lisa D'Amico' that was endorsed over to her as 'Lisa Daubman' and frankly, I don't know that I believe either of those names. It all seemed hokey as hell. The desk asked me about it and I told her that we don't cash third-party checks, and that she should maybe try a bank."

"Nicely played. But I'm sure that's not your only reason for inviting us?"

"It's not. I'm about to send some business your way, if you're okay with it. You won't guess who."

"Okay, who?"

"Alex Daubman. Is that going to be a conflict of interest for you?"

I exchanged a look with Dot, giving her the slightest nod.

"We're fine," she said. "We're not working for Lisa any longer."

"Besides, I'm not sure I even believe they're married," I added. "But some of the things she told us, we might have to keep those confidential from him."

"What does he want?" asked Dot.

"He says his wife is missing and he's worried about her. He asked if I could recommend a private investigator," replied Sam.

"Wow. You know anything about this situation from your end?"

"Yeah, a little. I did some digging. She left Friday night, around nine, with a small yellow suitcase. The concierge put her into a taxi. Alex had left about 15 minutes earlier, looking angry, according to the desk clerk. And one of the domestic staff said she'd heard an argument from their room earlier, when she was doing the evening rounds. He came back after midnight, more than a little drunk. Nobody remembers seeing her come in at all, and I haven't seen her since then."

"Geez, you sound like a freakin' detective!" I said.

He laughed loudly.

"Does Daubman know you're sharing all this with us?" I asked.

"Nope. I got a nasty feeling this is a domestic violence thing and I'm not going to help him out with that. I also didn't mention you'd been here already scoping out Lisa Whoever. I'll watch to see if he jumps when I mention your names, but I don't think he knows you're already involved with his so-called wife."

Dot jumped in. "Can you ask Daubman to come over later this afternoon? Say, three o'clock? We should be free then."

"Sure," said Sam. "He gave me his number at the studio and asked me to make it as soon as possible."

"Why so late?" I asked Dot. "We're free all afternoon."

"Because I want to do a couple of things first. One of them we should have done days ago." She looked at Sam. "Do you suppose you could let us into Daubman's room?"

Sam thought about that for a few moments. "Okay," he said, "but if anybody catches you in there, I'm going to deny letting you in."

"Fair enough," I replied. "We owe you one."

"Nah," he replied. "We're even. But if you offer to buy me a glass of wine or a cigar sometime, I won't say no."

Sam refilled our glasses and that was the last of the business talk.

Once Sam had signed the check, he led us across the lobby to the elevators. One of the operators stood up, but Sam waved him off. He stepped into the elevator with us and it felt like he took up as much space as the two of us together. He took us up to the third floor and opened Daubman's door with his passkey.

"Let me know when you're done," he said, "and I'll come back to lock up again." He turned away and headed back down to the lobby.

The room was decent enough, but not elaborate. It was large enough for two beds, only one of which had been slept in. There were also two bedside tables, two decent-sized wardrobes, and a vanity. Sure enough, there was a phone on the vanity. Through an open door on the wall opposite the bed, I could see a bathroom.

"What are we looking for?" I asked.

"I'm not really sure. A better idea of who these two people really are, what their relationship is. Anything out of the ordinary. Ideally, we want to find out what game they're playing, but I'm not expecting a miracle."

"Fair enough. I'll take the table and wardrobe on the far side, if you get this side."

I opened the bedside table. It held a pair of gold cufflinks, a packet of Chesterfields, and a small tin of rubbers. Clearly this was his side of the bed. The wardrobe on this side was also obviously his. It held two suits, both of them as smart as the one we'd seen him wearing, a number of ties, all silk, and half a dozen cotton button down shirts. There was a drawer at the bottom of the cupboard, which held undershirts, shorts, socks, and no surprises. I wondered what he wore when he wasn't wearing a suit.

I reported all this to Dot and it meant as little to her as it did to me. Her side of the room was not much more revealing. The smart suit we'd seen Lisa wearing before was in the closet, as were another equally well-tailored one and a couple of stylish dresses for evening wear. The two cheap dresses we'd seen her wear were missing.

"What do you think?" Dot asked.

"I think she took her own clothes and left behind the ones he bought for her," I said.

Dot checked the bathroom. "I don't see a toothbrush or a hairbrush for her, but she left behind the expensive perfume," she reported.

"We should get out of here before anybody gets back," I said.

We didn't get the chance. A key rattled in the lock and found the door already unlocked. The door knob turned and the door opened slightly, and through a narrow gap stepped a short, skinny man, not much taller than my 5'5". He looked to be half-ferret on his father's side, and was wearing a cheap-looking brown suit that fit so badly it was probably borrowed. In his hand, he held an automatic pistol, although he didn't seem to be pointing it anywhere in particular. My own Detective Special .38 was sitting uselessly in the purse dangling from my shoulder. We all stared at each other.

Dot reacted first. "What are you doing in our room?" she demanded angrily, hands on hips.

I wished I'd thought of that. He looked completely thrown. He wrestled with it for a couple of seconds.

"207?" he said uncertainly.

"209!" yelled Dot. "Get out!"

He twisted his body, leaned a little back and looked sideways at the outside of the half-open door. He straightened up.

"You lyin' b——" he said. That was as far as he got before my blackjack smacked into his temple. He dropped his gun, took a step sideways, and went down like a puppet with its strings cut. At that moment, a large figure filled the doorway. It was Sam, puffing heavily. He pushed the door fully open, rolling the ferrety man aside in the process.

"Looks like you have this under control," he said, a little breathlessly. He bent down, scooped up the pistol, and pocketed it. He took the ferret by the scruff of his jacket, pulled him upright, and shook him gently until he had his attention.

"An armed man in the room of two ladies? I could shoot you in the back right now and no jury in America would convict me," said Sam. "So you'd better have a good story."

The ferret cursed Sam out in a way I hadn't heard since I

hung around airmen. Sam smacked him so hard across the ear, his knees buckled before he caught himself and straightened.

"Watch your goddamn language in front of the ladies, asshole!" he told him.

I suppressed a giggle.

"Sorry to be a little late," Sam said to the two of us. "I saw this guy head up the stairs and thought he looked off. I had to take the elevator, though. I'm not built for running up stairs. I did run down the corridor, though."

"How did you know he'd come here?" I asked.

"My instincts said he was looking for trouble, and you two seem to be some sort of trouble magnets. So that was my first guess. No offense."

"What do we do with him now?" Dot asked.

"Well, that's a thing," said Sam. "If we involve the police, they're going to want to know what you two were doing in here, and they might get curious about how you sapped this guy, and that all gets complicated." Sam was right about that: my blackjack was completely illegal, and using it could even cost me my license. I resorted to it only when absolutely necessary.

"And I can't throw him down the stairs to the lobby, since that'd be bad for the hotel's reputation," Sam continued. "Probably best if I just take this bum out back and firmly explain to him why he shouldn't show his face in my hotel again."

"Thanks, Sam," I said. "You're a treasure. We definitely owe you now."

"You two better amscray before anybody comes to

investigate the noise," he replied. "I hope you got what you were looking for."

By the time we got back to the office, my adrenaline had mostly subsided. A fresh coffee and a Lucky Strike settled what remained of my nerves.

"Did we get what we were looking for?" I asked Dot, echoing Sam's words.

"Not really, although we learned that this business is a lot more complicated than we thought," she replied.

"And possibly more dangerous," I added.

"I could go a lot of ways", continued Dot. "The simplest is that Daubman knows nothing about what Lisa does during the day, and the gunman works for whoever killed your father. He could be looking for Lisa, or he could be working with Lisa. What he's doing in the room is anybody's guess, but I don't think it was about us."

"Or maybe he had been working with Lisa but she double-crossed him once she got the quitclaim, and he was looking for a lead on her. What's number two?"

"Yes, that's good. Two, Daubman is a potential buyer for the property, but doesn't know what Lisa did to get it, and doesn't want to. Maybe the guy was watching the room on Daubman's behalf, in case Lisa came back."

"He must want it badly to still be looking for Lisa. Because I don't believe for a moment they're really married."

"Third possibility is Daubman is in it up to his neck, and Lisa reneged on their deal after getting him to do the dirty work. Either way, it seems like a lot of trouble for him over a piece of property that doesn't seem like it's very valuable and won't turn much profit. He doesn't dress like he's hurting for money. Nothing here makes sense."

"I'm certainly not ready to let Daubman off the hook yet. I think it's about time we knew more about him."

I pulled a business card from my top drawer and started dialing.

"Who are you calling?" asked Dot.

"Eddie. He said he'd look into Daubman."

Dot picked up her extension.

Eddie answered on the third ring.

"Hey Detective Ramirez," I said. I figured I should keep it formal in case anybody else was listening in. "Joy here and Dot's on the line too. Did you find anything on our friend Daubman?"

"Not much, but what I did find was interesting. In the last couple of years, he's had a bunch of low-grade traffic tickets, but they all got fixed."

"What does 'fixed' mean?" asked Dot.

"It means somebody in the department dismissed them."

"Who can do that?"

"More or less anybody in Traffic division at the level of Captain or higher. Or somebody lower down with the balls to sign a Captain's name to it. Or another cop who's owed a favor could ask for it to be done. It's the kind of favor that gets done for friends, family, and celebrities all the time and nobody even blinks. But it gets better. A year or so ago, there was a serious assault charge against him, accusing him and an unnamed associate of beating a guy really badly. Premeditated too. It wasn't just some bar fight. And that also went away."

"What was the reason for dropping it?" I asked.

"That's the thing. There isn't one. The investigation just

stopped, and the case was closed. That takes a lot more pull than getting a traffic ticket erased."

"Huh. Sounds like Daubman has friends on the force."

"Yes, and here's the other thing. Before two years ago, there's nothing on him at all. His driver's license was issued in '44. Maybe that's just when he got his first car and started parking it carelessly, or maybe there's more there."

"Thanks, Eddie," I said. We ended the call.

"I have one more idea, but it's a long shot," said Dot. She picked up the phone and placed a call to our friend Ginnie Townsend.

I picked up my extension too.

"Hey Ginnie, how's life at the Marmont?" I asked, because I knew Dot wouldn't. Ginnie had managed to find a buyer for her rambling Victorian mansion a couple of months previously and was now living full time in an apartment at the Marmont Hotel.

"It's wonderful, dear!" she said. "I have all the space I need and none of the draughts I don't. I can get service any time of the day or night without any of the hassles of employing staff of my own. And the food here is a lot better than my cook was serving."

"What about the cars, though?" asked Dot. Ginnie had owned a beautiful 1942 Lincoln Continental, one of the last produced before the automakers had switched to wartime production, and an even more gorgeous midnight blue Cadillac 62 Coupe. I knew make and model because Dot had mentioned them admiringly many times.

"I let the Continental go," replied Ginnie. "I don't have a driver any longer. I kept the Coupe though, as they have a garage here and valet parking. And when I don't want to drive myself, I can just jump in a taxi. It's so convenient!"

"I hate to cut this off, but this isn't just a social call," said Dot. "Do you know anything about a man called Alex Daubman?"

"Is this about a case? Exciting! I do know an Alex Daubman, but not well. Tall, well-built, very sharply dressed, quite good-looking and knows it. We go to some of the same social events. He likes the horses."

"That sounds like him. What can you tell us?"

"He first showed up on the social circuit about two years ago. He works for Mammoth Pictures," she said. Dot and I looked at each other, both of us with our eyebrows raised. "His business card says something vague like President of Production Operations, but in reality, he is some sort of fixer."

"What does that mean?" asked Dot.

"He takes care of the studio and its actors, makes sure nothing bad happens to them or is written about them. Say one of the gossip sheets gets something juicy about one of Mammoth's stars, Daubman will persuade them not to print it. Maybe he'll pay them back with a promise of an exclusive interview with somebody big, or special access at a premiere. Or if a star gets into a drunken fight and is tossed in gaol, he'll bail them out and keep it quiet. If a starlet gets pregnant and has to leave town for a little while to get it taken care of, he'll make the arrangements. Basically, whatever needs doing to keep Mammoth looking good. Every studio has somebody like him."

"And I assume none of the other executives ever want to

know how it's done, right?"

"Absolutely. Clean hands. He's paid to be the cut-out. And as necessary as he is to them, he's not particularly welcome in their social circles."

"What about his wife?" I asked.

"As far as I know, he's not married," replied Ginnie. "Or if he is, his wife is remarkably tolerant about the string of pretty starlets he brings to parties and premieres."

"Any reason then he would be holed up in a hotel with a woman?"

"Actually, that's quite normal for men like him. They don't bring their girlfriends home, in case it gives them ideas about leaving their stockings to dry in the bathroom. That's just one step away from moving in permanently."

"Nice guy," I replied.

"It also keeps them away from staff who might sell the information to the gossip rags. I know what that's like."

"Thanks Ginnie, that's been very useful," said Dot. We made our goodbyes, promising to get together for cocktails the following week, and hung up.

"What do you think about Daubman now?" I asked Dot.

She stared at the wall for a minute. "I'm going to rule out him knowing nothing at all. Lisa has a piece of property right next door to Mammoth and she's sleeping with a guy who works for Mammoth? That seems like too much coincidence, and you know I don't like coincidences. It seems plausible Daubman is a buyer for Lisa's deed, or was, till she ran out on him. But to say he killed your father, or had him killed, that still feels like a big leap."

"I still can't figure what Daubman's angle would be in all

this," I said. "I assume he's buying it on behalf of Mammoth, but why does Mammoth want the land that badly? And why be so cloak-and-dagger about it?"

"I don't get it either, and that's one reason I have a hard time seeing him as the killer. It seems like an awful lot of risk over saving a few thousand dollars, and it's not even his money, it's Mammoth's."

"So what about Lisa? How deep in this do you think she is? Is the tail wagging the dog, or the dog wagging the tail?"

Dot turned that over for some seconds. "Hard to say. She definitely needs the money, even if the story she brought us isn't true, and maybe she fingered her own father for whoever killed him. That would be pretty cold, however estranged they were, but I could believe she was the one who got him drunk and drugged with the bourbon. I don't think she physically participated in the hanging itself, though. Or needed to. Perhaps she got him to open the door, then scooted over to the drugstore while it was happening, setting up whatever alibi she needed. Or maybe the way it played out was that she told Daubman the deal was scotched because her father was still alive, and then he took care of it without telling her in advance. I'm less sold on that version though."

"So either Daubman is deeply concerned about his missing wife, which I wouldn't buy for a plugged nickel, or he's chasing a sketchy real estate deal with a murder attached. Now I'm not sure I even want to find Lisa for Daubman. Maybe they deserve each other, and maybe they don't. The only thing keeping me on the case is the chance of finding out who killed my good-for-nothing father."

"Why do you want to know?" asked Dot, direct and to the

point as always.

"I want to have a complete story to tell my mother when I write to her."

"Fair enough. And this way we can keep track of him until we know more. Keep your friends close and your enemies closer, as the saying goes."

"Which one of those is Daubman?" I asked.

"I'm not sure yet," said Dot. "How about this? We listen to Daubman's story, and if there are no obvious alarm bells, we do our best to find Lisa and see what she has to say for herself. Then we decide what to tell Daubman."

"There's another thing. If Daubman killed my father, he can't miss the fact that Lisa and I have the same last name. He has to be at least curious about that, if not, downright suspicious."

Dot stared off and thought about that for a minute. "He won't bring it up. He has to pretend she's his wife, and he won't want to admit he knows anything about the property or the murder. And he probably wants to know as much about you as you do about him. So she's just going to be Mrs. Daubman, as far as we're concerned."

"I just don't want us to become loose ends that Daubman decides needs fixing."

"Just remember the first rule of intelligence," said Dot. "We don't admit to knowing anything about Daubman or Lisa that he doesn't tell us first."

Chapter Thirteen

Daubman showed up at three precisely. I wondered if he had been standing outside with an eye on his Rolex, waiting for the moment to make his entrance. He was as sharply dressed as the first time we had seen him, in a light gray double-breasted suit that was cut exactly according to this Fall's fashion, a pale blue shirt, an electric blue tie, and a matching pocket handkerchief. His cufflinks and tie pin were gold. His shoes were patent leather and looked handmade. Up close, he was evenly tanned, or perhaps naturally that dark, with a Roman nose and eyebrows that had been professionally tweezed and trimmed. His hair was immaculate. I wondered if he had to pay for grooming, or whether the studio's hair and makeup professionals took care of it as a perk of the job.

We sat at Dot's desk, with me alongside Daubman. We'd agreed that Dot would lead the interview, and I would mostly watch Daubman's reactions to see if they gave anything anyway. Dot handed him a sheet of paper.

"This is our standard contract," she said.

"Do we have to have paperwork?" he replied. "I'd like to keep this extremely discreet."

To my astonishment, Dot took the contract back and put it in her top drawer. I'd never seen her agree to work without a contract before. I didn't say anything, though. I assumed she had a reason, like she had for everything she did, and that I would find out later.

"We are known for our discretion, but okay. We charge 35 dollars a day each, plus reasonable expenses, and the clock is running. Mr. Lowry said your wife is missing, but nothing more."

"That's right. We have been staying at the Belvedere while our house is being decorated. On Friday night, we had an argument, and I stormed out. I needed to walk around to clear my head."

"I have to ask, did you harm her physically in any way? Because it's a cast iron rule for us that we will not help a husband in those circumstances."

"Absolutely not, I swear."

"Okay. Just be aware, if we find evidence to the contrary, confidentiality goes out the window and we're going to take it to the police. If you're not comfortable with that, now would be the time to leave. So what was the argument about?"

"Money, as always. She wanted more of it. Anyway, a walk turned into a drink, then some more drinks, and by the time I got back, it was midnight and I was plenty drunk. She wasn't there, and I went straight to bed."

So far, this story matched what Sam had told us.

"Were you worried when you found her gone?" Dot asked.

"No, because it's happened before. When we argue badly, sometimes she goes off to spend a day or two with a friend to let us both cool off, and then she comes back."

I was impressed. Either they really were a married couple, or he had done good work on his backstory.

"Anyway, in the morning, I still wasn't worried. I saw she had taken only a small suitcase and a few of her clothes, the ones easiest to pack, I guess. It seemed she wasn't planning to stay away for long."

"When did you start to worry?"

"Yesterday afternoon. She has never stayed away that long before, and I thought she would have at least called. I started to think that maybe something had happened to her. So I talked to the house detective and he recommended the two of you."

Dot put her pen down and leaned back a little. "This won't be easy. It gets much harder to find somebody after the first 24 hours have passed. A trail can go cold very quickly. But we can try. Let's take down some details." She picked up her pen again and sat forward. "What is your wife's name?"

"Lisa."

"Any last name she might be using?"

"Her maiden name was Brown."

That was interesting lie, and I wondered whose lie it was, Lisa's or Daubman's.

"Description?"

"5'6", about 120 pounds, straight blonde hair, turquoise eyes. Very pretty."

I wouldn't have called her pretty myself, but tastes vary, I guess.

"Will this help?" he continued. He pulled a black and white 8x10 photo from his briefcase. It was Lisa, glammed up for a Hollywood headshot. I wondered if he'd tried to sweeten her up with a promise of a screen test. I had to admit, the camera did love her.

"Any idea what clothes she took with her?"

"A floral print dress and a plain yellow one are definitely missing. But I don't know everything she owns. What husband does? And she has some cash, so she could be wearing something else entirely by now."

"Any known contacts? You mentioned a friend she sometimes stays with."

"I only know her first name, which is Joannie. And I don't know how to contact her. Unfortunately, I don't know any of her other friends. We lead very separate social lives."

The latter at least was true, I thought.

"I want to set your expectations low," said Dot. "If she doesn't want to be found, she could be long gone by now, especially with so little to go on. And to be clear, we get paid for our time, whether we find her or not. Also, if we're going to work without a contract, we're going to need a retainer. Three hundred dollars to start, and we'll contact you if we need more."

I was shocked at the number Dot had named, and tried not to show it. She always had a reason, and maybe she was testing Daubman to see whether he'd try to negotiate the number down. But Daubman simply nodded impassively, reached into his coat pocket and pulled out a wallet. Opening it, he retrieved three crisp, unfolded, hundred dollar bills. He laid them on the table, and fanned them out with all of the finesse of a professional poker dealer, then swept them back into a neat stack. He was probably walking around with a thousand dollars cash in his pocket. From another pocket in the wallet, he pulled a business card and laid it precisely on top of the money.

"That's my direct phone number at the office," he said. "It's for conversations I don't want the switchboard listening in on. Call me as soon as you have something."

"Thank you, Mr. Daubman," said Dot, and stood up.

Daubman and I did the same. We said our goodbyes and I showed him to the front door. A red Hudson coupe was parked across the street, trying to look as inconspicuous as a red coupe can manage.

I came back to the office and sat down across from Dot.

"Pick the bones out of that," she said.

"Three hundred dollars!" I said. "That was pushing it a bit, wasn't it?"

"Now we know he wants to find her very badly."

"You know, it is possible they really are married. In which case, I wouldn't want to be Daubman's next of kin and the owner of a valuable deed. That sounds like the makings of a short life expectancy. Maybe that's why she rabbitted."

"Nothing would surprise me at this point, not even somebody telling us the truth."

"Can I try telling the story?" I said.

"Go ahead."

"Let's suppose it's Lisa and Daubman working together, and try to figure out the third party angle later. The way I see it, Lisa gets hold of the deed when Emma dies. Accident, suicide, murder, I don't think we'll ever know unless she cops to it. Now she needs to cash in the deed with either Twentieth or Mammoth, but she knows only enough about real estate deals to know there's normally a lot of scrutiny around titles. Maybe she worries about the deed still being in her father's name."

"Possible. When she came to us, she certainly didn't know anything about the process," said Dot.

"Sure. So somehow, she gets in touch with Daubman, knowing he's some kind of shady. She tells him her poor orphan sob story and says she'll sign a contract for the lot at a discount right now, provided there's no questions asked. He agrees. He can buy it on behalf of Mammoth without anybody else looking closely. Or if he's feeling really slick, he buys it himself at a discount and then sells it on to Mammoth at full price, and they both make out. Maybe he doesn't know what Lisa's issues are, but he suspects something is iffy enough that Lisa can't go straight to Mammoth with no credibility."

"Right. So what he brings to the deal is his credibility with Mammoth. Good so far," said Dot. "But how do we get involved?"

"Okay, so Lisa brings the deed to Daubman and his lawyer to sign the paperwork, and they see it's in Tony's name, not hers or even her mother's, which she hadn't mentioned. She explains that her mother is dead and her father has abandoned them, so it belongs to her now. And that's when the lawyer tells her it's not enough for him to be missing, and instead, there has to be an effort to find him. He sends her off to take care of that, thinking it will be routine, because for him it would be.

"Meanwhile, Daubman puts her up at the Belvedere so she won't be homeless, buys her some nice clothes, and gives her a little walking around money from time to time. It's just enough to keep her on a short leash. But other than that, she's broke, and of course she has no idea how to do a search for her father that will satisfy a judge."

"So the part of her story about needing an investigator for free is true, and presumably she saw your name somewhere and figured out the connection," interjected Dot.

"Yes, I think I actually believe that part. She must have heard about my father's first marriage from her parents. When you're running a con, a small truth can help a big lie go down. And judging by his reaction—or lack of reaction—when he was here, I'm confident Daubman has no idea who we are or that she's been to see us. Either that or he plays his cards as close to his vest as you do. Anyway, everything is going fine until the whole plan went belly up when instead of proving her father is dead, we find him alive. Now Lisa has to go back to Daubman with the bad news that she has nothing right now and only half the property when he eventually dies. So Daubman decides to fix the problem immediately in his own special way."

"With or without her prior knowledge, we don't know."

"Sure, depending on how guilty you think she is," I said.

"Now with her father dead, everything is good again. In fact, it's even better than before. The quitclaim means they don't have to bother with probate court and Lisa doesn't have to split the proceeds with you. But that leaves one big question: why argue?" asked Dot.

"Why do thieves ever argue? Money. One of them decides they want a bigger cut. Or Lisa sees a chance to cut Daubman out entirely, and maybe sell it directly to the highest bidder. So now she's just laying low until things cool down. Either way, I don't believe it was just a spat. I think she's left him for good."

"Why?"

"She took all her own things, and none of his, or even the things he bought for her. To me, that says she doesn't want to give him any reason at all to pursue her. She's hoping he'll cut his losses. He has better things to do. But he can't do that, if she knows he committed murder."

"Do you think Joannie exists?"

"No. I think Daubman's had his own people looking for Lisa since first thing Friday morning, and he came to us because they turned up nothing. He just needed a story for why he waited this long."

"Excellent," said Dot. "I don't think I could have told it better myself."

I blushed at the compliment. "Hey, I learned it from watching you."

"Thank you. But here's another version. It all happened the way you said, except instead of telling Daubman that Tony was alive, she had it taken care of herself so she could come back to him with a clean title. He doesn't know how she did it, and he doesn't want to."

"You're right, that works too. I have to stop thinking the guy is guilty just because he's so sleazy. I wish I had your brain."

"It's a blessing and a curse, trust me."

"Still, a lot of things about this business are not making sense to me. One of them is why everybody is lying to us. There has to be more to the story."

"Maybe if we can find Lisa, she'll clear it all up. Mind you, we've still got very little to go on. Chances of finding her are slim."

"It's too late to do anything useful today," I said. "Let's make a fresh start in the morning."

We headed out for an early dinner and took our time eating, then over to Jack's for a drink or two. Sometime after seven, Dot started getting antsy, tapping her foot on the chair rail and drumming her fingers on the table. It very quickly got under my skin.

"What's up?" I asked, more in hope of getting her to stop than because I really wanted to know. I just wanted to have a quiet drink and go home.

"We need to know more about Daubman. Who was he before he came to Mammoth? He's a big mystery right now and he's got to be at the center of this mess, I'm increasingly sure of it," she grumbled.

I was surprised. I hadn't seen a case get to Dot like this before. Mind you, I hadn't seen a case that was such a house of mirrors before either. It had to be nagging at that orderly brain of hers.

"It sure feels like we're fumbling around in the dark. But what are we going to do? Follow him to work and sit outside the studio gates all day? I don't see how we're going to find anything Eddie couldn't."

"Mammoth must know more about their fixer. Surely, they didn't hire him without a thorough background check."

"How does that help? Do you think they'll show you his personnel file if you just walk in there and ask nicely?"

"I wasn't planning on asking at all," replied Dot with a dangerous smile.

It took a moment for the penny to drop. "You're planning to break in? That's crazy! Studios have tons of security!"

"Not at night. Security's there to keep the fans and the gossip writers out during working hours. There won't be much more than a guard on the gate and a couple of night watchmen after hours."

"And there will be locked doors and filing cabinets to deal with."

"Nothing we haven't dealt with before," she said confidently. "Finish your drink and let's go."

"Are you even listening to me?" I said exasperatedly. Her calmness deeply worried me. "I don't agree with this at all."

"Why not?"

"Because it's reckless and dangerous, that's why not. If Daubman finds out, it could wreck everything. And we have no idea what he's capable of."

"So you're out?"

"Darn right I'm out! And don't even think about going it alone!"

Suddenly I noticed the bar had grown quiet. Other tables were staring at me. Apparently, I'd been shouting. I blushed deeply. As far as I could remember, I'd never raised my voice to Dot before. But this plan was insane.

Dot looked at me coldly for several seconds, drained her rye, stubbed out her cigarette, and left.

I sat and stewed over my beer for ten minutes. I couldn't believe she was doing something so risky. I couldn't believe I had shouted at her. And most of all, I couldn't believe I was about to get up and follow her. Even though I was still furious, I knew I couldn't let her go alone. Somebody had to take care of her, and tonight it was me.

Outside, I waved down a cab. If Dot was taking streetcars, I might even get there before her. But if she'd taken a cab too, I was ten minutes behind.

We caught some traffic as we crossed into Hollywood and I was anxious I would miss her. The cab finally dropped me about a block from the main entrance to Mammoth. The gates were closed. Two watchmen were sitting in a brightly lit guard booth. Obviously, Dot wouldn't try to get in that way. Everything else was dark. Not even moonlight broke up the shadows.

Now that I was here, I had no idea how I was going to find Dot. I was standing there, feeling like I was on a fool's errand, my emotions some mix of anger at Dot and fear for her safety, when I caught movement out of the corner of my eye. I turned just in time to see a figure slip into an alleyway a hundred feet up the street. I followed as fast as I could walk. I wanted to call out to her, but I couldn't risk alerting somebody else.

The alleyway led down the side of Mammoth's lot. Halfway down, the figure stopped and started fiddling with something, a darker shadow inset into the dark of the wall. It had to be a side gate—maybe the studio used it to smuggle people in and out when they wanted to avoid the main gate. And that had to be Dot picking the lock. A moment later, she disappeared into the darkness. I hurried after. Inside the doorway, I spotted a three story brick building that looked to be full of offices. I could hear Dot's footsteps tapping on the sidewalk, and hoped nobody else could hear them. I slipped off my shoes so I could follow more quietly. After the way I'd shouted at her in the bar, I really didn't want to be the one who got us caught.

The door to the office opened to her just as easily as the gate had done, and she disappeared into the building. Suddenly, I noticed a light on the second floor. It flashed out of one window, then another. It had to be a night watchman making his rounds. Unbelievable, Dot, I thought. You're going to get us both tossed in jail. Or worse.

Behind a reception desk, there were three corridors, all unlit, branching off the lobby. I stood there uncertainly, wondering which one she'd taken, when I caught the beam of a pen flashlight to the left. I followed down the hallway as she turned the corner. I wondered if she had any idea where she was going, or if she was just going to wander around, looking for a door with Personnel painted on it.

I reached the end of the hallway and turned into another corridor. No sign of Dot. Left and right more corridors branched off of it. I had no idea which one Dot might have taken. Suddenly, the wall opposite one the corridors lit up brightly, and Dot's shadow was thrown monstrously against it from floor to ceiling. I heard a voice call out.

"Stop right there, miss!" it said. The voice sounded old and wheezy.

Dot's shadow shrank to human proportions as the flashlight approached her. I crept silently up to the corner and heard the man's voice again.

"What are you doing in here, miss? Do you work here? Do you have your badge?"

Dot didn't immediately answer.

Great, I thought. She's going to do something really dumb, like tell him the truth.

I was stuck. How was I going to get her out of this? I didn't want to sap an old man just for doing his job, and if I pointed my gun at him, it might give him a heart attack. I realized I was going to have to do something I would hate myself for later: act girlish. I stepped into the corridor behind

Dot and stood in the glare of the watchman's flashlight.

"There you are!" I said. Dot turned and stared at me in wide-eyed surprise.

"Two of you!" said the watchman, a white-haired man in his sixties or seventies in a baggy security guard uniform with an ersatz police badge pinned to it.

"Thank you, sir," I said, flashing my best smile and hating myself on the inside. "I thought I lost her. These corridors are a maze!"

"What are you up to?"

"I have a confession," I said as plaintively as I could manage. "We're writers for Modern Screen. We were trying to get some inside info on Hedy Lamarr, and this seemed like a good idea at the time. Now, not so much."

Dot managed to keep a straight face at my absurd story.

The watchman chuckled. "Ladies, you're in the wrong studio. Lamarr is at MGM."

"Oh, gosh, now I feel silly," I said. I thought about trying to fake a girlish giggle, but I didn't think I'd have it in me. I was embarrassing myself enough already. "I guess we should leave."

He scratched behind his ear. "Well, I don't know if I can just let this go." He rested his hand on the bulky walkie-talkie on his belt. War surplus, I guessed.

I pulled out my wallet and looked inside. "Would ten bucks help you forget about it?" I asked. I guessed he probably made less than a buck an hour.

He gave that a couple of moment's thought. "I could be quite forgetful for ten bucks, I suppose. And I guess you two little ladies seem more foolish than dangerous. I'll show you out the side gate."

I choked down my irritation and handed over the money. Thirty minutes later, we were sat in the back of a small jazz club about three blocks from Mammoth, with large drinks in front of us. I lit up a Lucky Strike and took a long draw. I hadn't said a word to Dot on the walk over, and she had wisely taken that as a clue she shouldn't speak either.

Finally, I broke the silence. "That was the dumbest thing I've ever seen you do. What got into you?"

"I'm sorry, truly," she said. "Especially about putting you in danger too. I got cocky. I should have listened to you. Can you forgive me?"

"Not yet," I said. "Least of all for making me have to put on that girlish nonsense."

"Sorry. You're right, that was the worst. When he called us 'foolish little ladies' I thought you were going to get your blackjack out. Thank you for restraining yourself."

I didn't want to, but I had to laugh at that a little. "Okay, I forgive you a tiny bit. But you're buying the drinks tonight. And you owe me ten bucks."

Chapter Fourteen

First thing Tuesday morning, I called the number in Inglewood where Lisa had said she was going to share an apartment. No surprise, nobody there had heard of Lisa D'Amico or Lisa Daubman, and they didn't have a room to let.

As I sat at my desk, trying to think of a useful next step, the outer door jangled, announcing a visitor. I went out into the waiting room to find an older gentleman there, his dark gray Derby hat in his hand. I tried to think when I'd last seen a man wearing a Derby. Before the war, probably. He had a nice quality, conservatively cut, three-piece suit in brown wool that was probably too heavy for LA's climate, with an old-fashioned watchchain across the vest. He was plump and round and soft all over with little wireframe glasses that made his face look even rounder. He was almost bald, except for two little tufts of gray over his ears. He was probably in his fifties, but the lack of hair made him look older.

"Are you Miss D'Amico or Miss Stone?" he asked. His voice was bright like a child that's been promised ice cream if it watches its manners.

"D'Amico," I replied.

"Good, it's you I need to see."

"I'm popular this month. Step into the office."

Dot looked up when we came in, saw nothing to interest her, and went back to her law book. The man waited for me to take my seat, then sat down across from me. He fished a card from his waistcoat pocket and handed it across the desk.

William Wetherby, Esq.

Attorney at Law

I read it, and disliked him immediately on principle.

"I won't take up much of your time," said Wetherby, "but I did want to meet you in person and invite you to have dinner with me tonight." He spoke a little timidly. I couldn't imagine him in court, but perhaps he wasn't that kind of lawyer. He reminded me of the smalltown lawyers I'd known growing up, the type that dealt with farm mortgages that often ended with the family losing the farm.

"If you're asking for a date, I'm sorry, but you're not my type," I told him. "If it's business, could we just deal with it here and now?" I had absolutely no desire to spend my evening with this man. On top of that, I had much better plans.

"It is indeed business. It's regarding the D'Amico property in Century City. I'm afraid I'm on my way to another appointment, so I was hoping you might be free this evening. Say, seven o'clock at Perino's?"

"I don't have anything to wear," I said.

"Don't worry, just do your best. I'll have a word with the maitre d' and make sure it isn't a problem," he said. I upped my evaluation of him from 'dislike' to 'hate'.

"Call me later, say around noon, and I'll let you know," I said. I didn't want to make a decision while I was angry.

"Very well," he said, and stood up. To my relief, Dot got up to show him out, allowing me to quietly seethe for a minute. By the time she came back and sat down across from me, I already had a cigarette going and a fresh cup of coffee.

"Lucky you. I heard the food at Perino's is fabulous. And such charming company, too."

"I'm going to have to cancel a date for this. Can you at least help me pick out an outfit that won't completely embarrass my host?"

"Of course. Well done, by the way," she said.

"For what?" I asked.

"Not smacking him. I probably would have."

"I wish he'd invited you too."

"Why?"

"Partly to restrain me from hitting him when he gets patronizing again. But also to let me know when I'm using the wrong fork."

Dot laughed, and I started to unwind a little.

"So what do you make of all that?" she asked.

"It seems like we do have another party interested in the property."

"I agree. On the other hand, I find it hard to see a lawyer like him and the ferret from the Belvedere moving in the same circles. So maybe we have three parties. Darn it, we need more information."

"Isn't Peroni's supposedly mobbed up?" I asked. "Maybe it's just a coincidence, but it wouldn't be unusual for the mob to have a legitimate-looking front office with lawyers and accountants and such."

"Conversely, it also wouldn't be unknown for a corporation to quietly hire a few thugs and lowlifes to do their dirty work," said Dot.

"Sometimes it's hard to tell one from the other," I replied.

"Meanwhile, we still have no handle on Lisa, and 300 dollars to earn. Any thoughts?"

"I'm up for some good old fashioned legwork to get me

out of my own head," I said. "I want to go over to Lisa's old neighborhood and ask around, see if I can turn up anything. Maybe she had friends there, or the neighbors know something. Somebody might even have heard of the mysterious Joannie, if she exists. Lisa could even have gone to ground there. After all, it's a place she knows and where she maybe feels safe."

"You're always happiest when you're on the move, aren't you? If you can handle that by yourself, I want to head back to City Hall. And not just for the coffee. I have a thought about something. Well, not really a thought yet, more of an itch, and it's probably going to take all morning in the Vital Records office to scratch it."

"Alright, I guess I'll maybe see you back here for lunch." There was no point asking Dot what her hunch was. She never liked to talk about her intuitions until she knew whether they had worked out or not.

It was a long, slow ride out to Claremont on a Yellow Car. Long enough that I took a seat for once. I rarely go that far east and I quickly lost count of how many stops we had made. Finally, I got off and walked three blocks north to Emma's old neighborhood, and found her street, which backed right on to a state highway. It was a series of clapboard houses that were little more than shacks. All of them were badly in need of a paint job and some of them looked like a good push would bring them down. As far as real estate goes, they would make decent firewood.

I found Emma D'Amico's address easily enough. It was no better and no worse than the shanties around it. It had a single window on the front, boarded up on one half. I knocked on the door and waited, but wasn't surprised when there was no answer. I walked over to the house next door and knocked there. The door quickly opened on a middle-aged woman with the face of poverty. She had dry, thin hair and was wearing a dressing robe worn shiny in places. "Can I help you?" she asked.

"I hope so. I'm a relative of the late Mrs. D'Amico," I said, which was more or less true. "I'm trying to find out some information about her life here before she died." I pulled my driver's license from my purse and showed it to her.

"Joy D'Amico," she said, reading from my license. "I'm Beth. Come on in."

The so-called house was just two rooms, maybe even smaller in total than Tony's apartment. There was only a cramped bathroom and a single room for everything else. The floor was rough wood, some of it covered by a faded woolen rug. She sat me down at the small table.

"Tea?" she asked.

"Please." I never drank tea, but I wanted to be polite.

"You take milk?"

"Oh, no, I'm fine."

"Good, because I don't have any."

I waited in impatient silence while she made the tea and poured a mug for each of us, then sat down at the table across from me.

"I should tell you right off that if you're looking for some kind of inheritance, you're in the wrong neighborhood. Other than that, what do you want to know about poor Emma, rest her soul?" she asked.

"How long had you known her?" I asked. I didn't want to

jump straight into questions about Lisa, in case she had told friends and neighbors here to watch out for snooping.

"I would have to say… ten years, I guess."

"Were you friends?"

"As much as neighbors ever are, I suppose."

"And you knew Tony too, from before he left?"

"Well, I wouldn't say I knew him well. He came and went at all hours. And then one day, he went and never came back. That was, oh, eight years ago?"

"Eight sounds right. And what about the daughter?"

Beth looked at me for a long second, confusion etched on her face. "She didn't have a daughter. She didn't have any kids at all."

Now it was my turn to be confused. "You don't know a skinny girl, blonde hair, distinctive blue-green eyes?"

"Do you mean Helen? Helen James? She lived in the neighborhood and used to come around a lot and help Emma out, doing chores and errands, especially on days when Emma couldn't get out of bed. Some people might say she was like a daughter to Emma, I suppose."

"Emma was sick?"

"She had something, it would come and go, that made her too tired to move. And it's not like she could afford to see a doctor about it, so she just put up with it. Maybe that's why she did what she did."

"What do you mean?"

"Took her own life. Maybe she just got too tired to keep going."

It sounded possible, I supposed.

"Does Helen still live around here?" I asked. "She might

be able to tell me more about Emma." I thought that wasn't a bad lie off the top of my head. And it didn't seem to make Beth wary.

"I don't think so. She was living in Emma's house towards the end, when Emma needed help pretty much every day. I haven't seen her around since a couple of weeks after Emma passed."

"Did she have any friends in the neighborhood? Somebody who might know where to find her?"

"She was mostly a very solitary girl. She had home and school and Emma. I guess there was one girl her own age she hung around with a lot, getting into mischief, whenever Emma didn't need her. The girl's name was Sheila Barron. But Sheila got out a couple of years ago, so that's likely not much help."

She was probably right, but I wrote it down anyway.

"Listen, you've been really helpful," I said, "but I should be getting out of your way."

"You've not touched your tea," she pointed out.

"That's okay, thank you," I said, getting up from the table.

"Never mind. I'll put it back in the pot for later," she said, and got up to open the door for me. I thanked her again and stepped outside.

I walked the neighborhood for about 30 minutes, looking at falling-down shacks with leaky roofs, and wondering how poor you had to be to not waste cups of tea. My head was full of thoughts, all chasing each other in circles. I didn't feel much like knocking on more doors and sitting in more dreary rooms just to find out more about Helen. The whole exercise was making me depressed and I was starting to think it had been a bad idea to come here at all. I walked back to the Yellow Line stop and waited for the long, slow ride back to the office.

I went out for lunch about noon and got back around half-past to find that Dot had returned while I was gone. She poured me a coffee and sat across my desk from me.

"Did you find anything interesting?" she asked.

"Interesting and surprising, although maybe in hindsight, I should have seen it coming. Lisa D'Amico is not really Emma's daughter. In fact, Emma didn't have a daughter at all," I said. "She might well be a girl from the neighborhood called Helen James, though. How did your hunch play out?"

Dot smiled. "I'll go you one better. Emma did have a daughter."

"The neighbor I talked to said she didn't," I said warily. Dot was rarely wrong when she was this confident.

"I spent the morning checking death records. I thought it was odd that your father never mentioned Lisa, even when we brought up Emma, and I had a hunch about why. Lisa D'Amico died when she was three, from pneumonia. Helen—or whoever—presumably heard the story from Emma. After Emma died, I imagine she came up with an idea for how she could get ownership of the deed. I think she requested a certified copy of the birth certificate, maybe even faked Emma's name on the request, and took the name for herself. It's a common enough trick if you want a new identity. You just have to hope you don't run into somebody who knows the truth about the dead person."

"How do you know about that?" I asked. My eyes must have been wide with astonishment.

"When I was working for Intelligence, there was another group of girls who created identities for undercover agents. They'd find suitable birth certificates from children who'd died young, use those to get driver's licenses and passports, and then create whole backstories for the agents with legitimate documents. Sometimes, they'd find candidates by wandering around cemeteries looking for graves of young children. It sounds morbid, but it was important work."

I felt like I didn't know even half of what Dot had seen during the war.

"Okay, that sounds plausible," I said. "She might even have found the original birth certificate in Emma's things after she died, and that started her thinking about ways to get hold of the deed. Now I'm wondering if Daubman knows that Lisa or Helen or whoever is not who she claims and is just going along with it to get the deed. Or maybe she's conning him too. In fact, the more we learn, the less of a handle on Daubman I have."

"I feel the same. I'm back to wondering if maybe the only thing he's guilty of is putting a desperate woman up in a hotel and taking advantage of her. That would make him a creep for sure, but not a criminal."

"And he might be keen to find her if she took something valuable with her on the way out, like an expensive watch or his diamond cufflinks. It's certainly a simpler explanation than mine. Did we just leap to an assumption because of the Mammoth Pictures connection and seeing Lisa and Daubman together?"

"You know how I feel about coincidences, but we should consider it. That would also mean we have no idea who murdered your father."

"Yeah, we're back to zero on that," I said glumly.

"It also makes the quitclaim moot. The real Lisa D'Amico is dead and Helen James has no claim. The property belongs to you now, or it will, once probate settles."

"Wow, you're right, I hadn't realized that," I said, wide-eyed. "Mind you, if James already sold it on, what happens then?"

"I expect you'd need to go to court to get it all disentangled, which unfortunately, could eat up a lot of what the property is worth."

"Yeah, probably. For about 30 seconds there, I felt rich." I slumped back in my seat.

"By the way, did you turn up anything else useful?" Dot asked.

"Oh, right, I almost forgot. The neighbor said that Helen had a childhood friend called Sheila Barron. I know it's a long shot, but we should at least run it to ground."

Dot went over to my bookshelves and pulled down the phone directory.

"There's two Sheila Barrons listed, plus a Sheila Baron with one 'r', and three more with an 's' on the end, as in Barrons. One of them could be ours."

I opened up the street map and we marked the addresses. It was 20 minutes away on a streetcar to the closest Sheila. The furthest one was maybe an hour in the other direction. It would have been a lot easier back when I had the use of a cab. As it was, we'd be spending a lot of time hopping on and off streetcars. It looked like hard work, but it was just basic legwork and doorstepping and persistence. It'd maybe take less than a day if we got lucky.

"Don't make any assumptions," said Dot. "It could be nothing, or maybe it's the wrong Sheila Barron entirely. Ours might not be in the book at all. Or not live in LA any longer. Or be married and we're looking in completely the wrong place. But it's better than nothing."

"Do you want to phone these people first to save us some wasted trips?"

"No. If Helen is there, I don't want to spook her. But I do want to confront her with the truth and see what happens. And possibly get your property back."

"Makes sense," I said. "Do you want to hit up a couple of them this afternoon, or start fresh tomorrow?"

"Let's do it tomorrow. I have some paperwork to wrap up so we can get paid, and then we have to pick out an outfit for your date."

Chapter Fifteen

I got to Perino's at about five minutes past seven. I spent the next five minutes standing across the street watching Wetherby fretting outside the door, pacing up and down, and repeatedly pulling his pocketwatch out, checking it, and putting it back in his vest pocket. I briefly considered walking away and taking another lap around the block just to wind him up some more, but he spotted me and waved me over.

He looked at my outfit critically. Dot had insisted that I buy a couple of outfits that would blend in when we had to work in professional settings, and I was wearing one of them. She had helped me select a deep blue cotton suit with a pencil skirt that fell just below the knee and had enough of a side slit that I could actually walk. The jacket had three buttons and Dot had instructed me to button only the top two, letting the bottom of the jacket flare out over my hips. Underneath, I wore a simple crisp, white cotton blouse. I had to concede it looked professional and smart, but it was nothing I would ever choose for myself. At least it wasn't some ridiculous evening dress.

"Thank goodness you're here," huffed Wetherby. "I was beginning to worry they might give away our table." I flinched as he put his soft, chubby hand in the small of my back. He steered me inside, nodding to the maitre d' as we reached his station. The maitre d' held his finger up for a moment while he checked his seating chart, then dispatched one of his underlings to show us to our table, which was actually a semi-circular booth that meant we could sit as close together as we wished. I took a seat on one end, hoping to place myself as far from Wetherby's puffy fingers as possible.

Wetherby turned away and waved to somebody at the bar. A man acknowledged him with a small gesture, drained his drink, got up from his stool, and wandered over. He was moderately tall, and appeared more so standing next to Wetherby. He was also very well built. His suit was sharp and his tie was narrow, and it seemed he could easily have shared a tailor with Daubman. His face was weathered. He might work in an office now, but he'd worked outside when he was younger. His hair was mostly dark but speckled with gray. He was in his late forties or early fifties, I guessed, and fairly distinguished-looking, if that was your type. I couldn't decide whether he looked more like a gangster or a banker. Or perhaps a banker to gangsters.

"Miss D'Amico, may I present my colleague, Mr. Logan?" said Wetherby.

Logan offered his hand and shook mine confidently. He had the longest, thinnest fingers I had ever seen on a man. The thought, a strangler's hands, popped into my head from nowhere, and I suppressed a shudder. We settled ourselves onto the bank seat and I found myself seated across from Logan, with Wetherby on his inside. It wasn't hard to figure out which of them was in charge.

"I didn't realize I could bring a date," I said. Neither Wetherby nor Logan seemed amused.

"Mr. Logan is responsible for business development," said Wetherby. He didn't say what kind of business.

"A pleasure to meet you, Miss D'Amico," said Logan. I detected a Texas accent, but not a strong one.

I gave the room the once over. It was big, and I guessed it

could hold anywhere from 100 to 150 people. The lighting was soft, provided by a combination of elegant wall sconces and ornate chandeliers, arranged so that the tables were lit gently and the spaces between hardly at all. The tuxedoed waiters practically vanished between tables. Ours arrived with menus and took our drinks orders. I asked for a Scotch, my go-to when beer isn't appropriate. Our attention focused on the menu for a few minutes. I'd never seen such a long menu in my life. The specials list alone was longer than the menu at most places I ate. I was feeling completely lost. I looked around for our waiter only to find he had already mysteriously materialized at my elbow. These people were good.

"Have you dined with us before?" he asked.

I shook my head. It was polite of him to entertain the possibility that I might have, despite the way I was dressed.

"Then I would suggest some of our signature items. Perhaps the liver paté, which is made in our own kitchens, and a side salad to start. Our salads are fresh every single day from a local market. And for the entrée, we are famous for our steaks, and the lobster is also excellent tonight." He had elegantly narrowed 150 entrées down to two.

I decided to take his recommendation of the liver paté. I'd never had it and had no idea if I'd like it, but I had a petty urge to stick Wetherby with a large check for ruining my date plans, and it was suitably expensive. For the entrée, I was briefly tempted by the lobster, a dish whose messiness would have terrified Dot, but settled on the steak.

"Interesting place," I said, taking in the scene more fully. "I hear it's popular with the mob." If I was hoping I might provoke a reaction, I was disappointed.

"It's also where Hollywood royalty eat," said Logan. "They say Bette Davis has a permanent reservation. If you see somebody you recognize, please don't make a fuss."

Logan and Wetherby made awkward small talk over the appetizers. The paté lived up to its billing and more. It was like eating cream cheese made of meat. I sipped the wine Logan had ordered. I felt sure it was hugely more expensive than the one Sam had treated us to at lunch, but I preferred his Californian to Logan's French. I guess I know nothing about wine.

Our plates vanished and our entrées arrived seamlessly. Finally, the conversation turned to business.

"As Mr. Wetherby mentioned, we're interested in acquiring the D'Amico property," said Logan. "We're aware that you're Tony D'Amico's daughter by his first wife."

"I think you should know that I don't own it," I replied. "It belongs to my half-sister, Lisa D'Amico."

"You're referring to the quitclaim found with Mr. D'Amico's body, I assume," said Wetherby.

"Yes, that's right," I said. I wondered how he knew this. I hadn't seen anything in the press about such a minor story.

"I think we both know that document will not stand up to scrutiny in court," said Wetherby. "Probably not the suicide note either, but that's a separate matter." Apparently, he'd had access to the entire police report. I filed that away for later consideration.

"Why would you want to challenge it, though? Isn't it easier to just let it go and make a deal with Lisa?"

Wetherby looked to Logan on that one. "Because she

won't deal with us. She has a commitment to… another party," he said.

"Do you mean Daubman?" I asked. "Or is there a third buyer involved?"

"Yes, Daubman," said Logan. He looked a little surprised I knew that. He might be even more surprised to hear that Lisa had run out on Daubman and was in play again. I briefly thought about telling him, but remembered Dot's rule not to share intelligence if you didn't have to. I still knew nothing about who these people were or why they wanted the land so badly, but at least I'd confirmed that Daubman was a player in this, even if I still didn't know what exactly his endgame was.

"Then I assume you also realize that if you get the quitclaim thrown out, I'll only own half of the property?" I said.

"Of course," said Logan, "but that, at least, gives us some leverage. We believe Daubman will sell his half to us, provided he makes a decent profit."

Clearly, they also didn't know Lisa's big secret, or they'd realize I was entitled to the whole thing. And then I had a thought Dot would be proud of. Perhaps they did know, but thought I didn't. And if they told me, I would be in a position to demand a much higher price. Perhaps they were following Dot's rule too. The possibilities made my head spin a little. Maybe nobody was fooling anybody here. I wished Dot was here to sort it all out.

"One thing is still bothering me. Why all the secrecy? I know Daubman works for Mammoth Pictures, but you haven't told me anything about who you are or who you represent or why anybody wants this scrap of land so badly."

Logan took a few seconds to compose an answer. "To put it as plainly as I can, the land has significant value to us that we don't want competitors to know about. We very much want to avoid a bidding war."

"It sounds like I should very much want a bidding war," I replied.

"Precisely," said Logan, "and that is why we won't answer your questions."

I sat back on the bench and looked him in the eye. "Okay. Let's get down to brass tacks. What's your offer?"

"Fifteen thousand dollars for your interest," said Wetherby, "contingent on the court ruling in your favor. We will deal with the legal side at our own cost and risk. The number is not negotiable." Assuming they had offered James the same for her half, that was significantly more than what she had thought she could get for the whole thing. That seemed like a good reason for her and Daubman to argue about money.

"What happens if I say no?"

Wetherby looked anxiously at Logan, who was apparently considering his words carefully. He pursed and unpursed his lips.

"Then we'll have to consider other business strategies," he finally said.

"But you're still picking up the check for dinner, right?"

Logan almost smiled at that.

"Listen," I continued, "if you're all done being mysterious, I'm not going to make a decision right now. I want to take a day or two. I have Wetherby's card, I'll call him when I've decided."

I sat forward and devoted my full attention to the steak. It was delicious.

Chapter Sixteen

The next morning, Dot and I met at the office. I relayed the conversation from dinner while she listened patiently and took notes.

"You should have stayed for dessert," Dot told me when I mentioned I had bailed after the main course.

"Not with that company," I replied. "When I'm rich, we'll go there with Ginnie and enjoy it properly."

"It sounds like they don't know who Helen really is, which is good for us. I suppose it's still possible they do know, but are willing to play along with the deception as long as it leads to them owning the property," she replied. "Or they plan to wait until you've signed over your rights, and then they'll out her, leaving them with everything for half price. There are just layers and layers of deception here. Of course, we could sink the whole thing at a stroke with what we know about Helen, and get you the whole property."

"I'm not sure how I feel about that. Somebody already committed murder to put the property in the name of Lisa D'Amico, and yesterday, somebody pointed a gun at us over it. Or at least, he waved a gun in our general direction before I took it off him. And I wonder how scared of Daubman Helen must be if she didn't take Wetherby's offer on the spot. That seemed like an easy out for her. If somebody knows I'm about to become the genuine owner of the deed, am I more likely to get rich or get killed?"

"Good point. And me as well, if they find out I also know the truth about Helen."

"I'm starting to think I should just take the offer right

now and walk away from this whole mess. I don't need to squeeze all the juice out of it, since it's already more money than I've ever had, and plenty enough for me."

"That would leave you safe, if you're okay with the settlement."

"And then finding Helen would be somebody else's business. She's told us nothing but lies since she walked in the door and she might even have helped get my father killed. We don't owe her anything." I thought Inside my head I sounded fairly convincing, but despite everything, my conscience was still nagging me about cutting Helen loose.

"I think that makes Helen safe, too," said Dot. "With one half sold to Logan, Daubman needs so-called 'Lisa D'Amico' alive and cooperative in order to get her half. That way, he can wring some kind of arbitrage out of this whole business. She has no heirs that we know of, so if she dies, her half will go to the state. And apparently, nobody wants that."

Despite Dot's logic, I still couldn't shake the feeling that Helen was going to find a way to get herself killed over a few thousand dollars. And she might get me killed too.

"We could just go public with who she really is, and then she's of no interest to anybody," I said.

"That works too," said Dot. "But potentially puts you back in danger. We have to tread very carefully. If somebody else figures it out too, and they think we're the only other people who know, they might come after us to secure Lisa's claim. So if we tell the story, we need to make sure lots of people hear it. That's our protection."

"Right, that's a decision. I'm going to call Wetherby before I change my mind again."

I called the number on the card Wetherby had left with me, and his secretary picked up. She told me his diary was full all day, but she would check with him whether something could be canceled, if I didn't mind holding. There was nothing but background static for a few moments before she came back.

"Mr. Wetherby asked whether you wouldn't mind coming at six o'clock?"

"I can do that," I replied.

"I'll be leaving at five, so you'll have to show yourself in. I'll leave the door unlocked for you. He assumes a check will be acceptable? We wouldn't have that much cash at short notice"

"That's fine."

After we had hung up, I turned to Dot. "If I cash the check, how big a bag will I need?" I asked. I'd never seen any amount of money remotely that large except in bank robber movies.

"In theory, it could fit in your wallet. It could be as few as three bills," said Dot.

"Seriously? There's a 5,000 dollar bill?"

"Yes. Madison is on it. But good luck spending it on anything cheaper than a car. Can you imagine asking a grocery store to make change?"

"I guess I'm going to have to open a bank account. That'll be a first for me."

"Don't worry, it's very straightforward, and bankers tend to be polite to people with large amounts of money. You could use the same bank we use for the business. I'll come with you if you like."

"Thanks. And will you come with me this evening too? Wetherby gives me the creeps and I don't want to be alone with him."

"Of course. I'll also feel better if you're not walking around with a 15,000 dollar check by yourself."

"And afterwards, we go to Jack's and celebrate, okay?" I said.

"Celebrate the windfall, or celebrate the end of this sordid business?" asked Dot.

"Both. Double celebration. Meanwhile, there's one more thing I want to wrap up."

"What's that?"

"The guy that's been tailing us is across the street again. It's time we found out what he's about."

I picked up the phone and made a quick call, then Dot and I waited for 15 minutes. We pulled on our coats and headed out, walking west. The man peeled himself off the wall and followed us. After a couple of blocks, we turned into an alley. Fifty feet or so into the alley we stopped and turned. He was about ten paces behind us.

"Hi there," I said. "Were you looking for us?"

He stood frozen for a moment, alarm written all over his face. Then he turned around as smartly as a soldier on parade, and bounced off Sam's broad chest. Sam really could move quietly for such a big man. He put his huge hand against the man's chest and pushed him up against the wall, leaning in enough to pin him there with his weight. With his free hand, he frisked him efficiently, coming away with a small automatic. Dot and I joined Sam.

Close up, I realized how young the man was, maybe

eighteen or nineteen at most. And he looked terrified.

"Okay kid, what's your story?" said Sam.

"Please don't hurt me, okay?" he bleated. "I'm a private detective, just like you."

"So why are you following us?" I asked.

"Daubman's girlfriend hired me to find out what he was doing in a hotel with another woman," he blurted out. "He's at work all day, so I started following the woman. When she disappeared, I figured you two might lead me to her."

"You're terrible at this business," I said. "We made you right away in the lobby of the Belvedere."

"And you need to get a less conspicuous car," added Dot. "That red Hudson coupe stands out like a circus parade."

The boy looked close to tears. "I did everything the way the book said," he whispered.

"The book?" I asked, baffled.

"Yeah. I took a correspondence course on how to be a PI, but none of it seems to work. It cost me every last penny of my savings. I think I got burned."

"Did the book tell you to carry a gun?" asked Sam.

"It's a movie prop," said the boy miserably. "I thought it might be useful if I had to threaten somebody. I could never shoot anyone."

Sam took his weight off the boy and stood him up straight. He looked thoughtful for a few moments.

"Listen kid, here's what's going to happen," he said. "You're going to go back to your client and tell her she doesn't have to worry, Daubman and the girl is all business. And you're going to let her pay you for two days' work." He paused. "And then on Monday, you're going to come and see me at the Belvedere and I'm going to teach you how to do this job properly."

The boy stared at Sam wide-eyed. "For real?"

"Sure," said Sam. "It's about time I had a sidekick. I'm getting too old to be on my feet all day. Now skedaddle."

Dot and I looked at Sam in amazement. Finally, Dot spoke.

"You're a good man, Sam. It's our turn to buy you lunch."

After lunch, we filled the rest of the day with regular work, although Dot seemed to be having an easier time focusing than I was. She went downtown to research some property tax records for an embezzlement case, and I spent a couple of hours following a wayward husband without catching him in anything compromising. Still, I was happier to be on the move than sitting behind a desk fretting. I was back at the office by 4:30 p.m. and spent the next half hour transcribing my shorthand notes about my target's movements and thinking about strategy for the next day. I watched the clock tick around to five, and then we locked up the office and headed out.

The streetcars were crowded at that hour as always, and the ride was slow and uncomfortable. We passed up a couple of over-crowded cars with people spilling out the doors and hanging off the boards, and got to Wetherby's building around 5:45 p.m. It was a somber four story brick building embellished with stone window sills and lintels, and it felt very appropriate for a corporate lawyer. We stepped onto the small porch and consulted the row of doorbells and their brass labels. Wetherby was on the third floor, sandwiched between two accountants. I pressed the buzzer to let him know we were there, and we headed inside and up the stairs. As we reached the third floor, I was surprised to find the landing light off, and all three offices dark behind their frosted glass. It felt wrong, and immediately, my anxiety spiked. Why would the light be out if Wetherby was expecting us?

I looked at Dot and put my finger to my lips, then slipped out of my shoes. Dot did the same, and I pulled my Detective Special from my purse. The little snub-nosed revolver felt heavier in my hand than in my bag, but I didn't want to be taken by surprise like I had been at the Belvedere. Dot and I crossed the dark hallway silently in our stockinged feet and positioned ourselves on either side of Wetherby's door, Dot nearest the handle. We waited a minute for our eyes to adjust to the dark, and I nodded to Dot when I was ready. She turned the handle carefully until the latch was clear, then pushed it away from her and let it swing open a few inches. I pointed my gun into the gap, held my breath, and listened intently.

Nothing.

I pushed and let the door swing open, then stepped inside as quietly as I could, Dot following close behind. We found ourselves in a reception room, presumably the one where I'd spoken to Wetherby's secretary. It looked like any reception room anywhere, with a few uncomfortable looking chairs, a coffee table, a coatstand, a neat desk with a phone and a typewriter. Behind the desk, the door to the inner office was closed. It was easy to imagine the secretary diligently clearing away her things, putting the dust cover over the typewriter, and wishing Wetherby a good evening before leaving.

Perhaps she had simply turned out the light on the way out from force of habit.

The cold lump in the bottom of my stomach and the pounding in my ears were not convinced. We padded across the rug to the inner door. I held my gun down by my side with my finger clear of the trigger, the way I'd been taught. I reached for the door handle and turned it slowly. The door eased open. Inside was a large leather-topped desk and behind it lay the sprawled body of Wetherby.

I pushed the door fully open and we both stepped inside. The moonlight from the window bisected his body, leaving his legs in deep shadow and illuminating the broad pool of blood that lay around his head like a dark halo.

"Are you ready?" asked Dot.

"Yes," I replied.

She turned on the lamp. Sickly yellow light fell over the scene. Wetherby was lying face down, his head turned in profile. I could see gashes to his hands and neck. Neither one of us felt like joking that we'd seen worse. We hadn't.

The safe stood open and empty with Wetherby's keys hanging from the lock.

We stepped back into the outer office and I turned on the light there. Dot found a handkerchief in her purse and wrapped it around the telephone before picking up the receiver and dialing.

"Detective Ramirez?" said Dot. "You're going to need to see this. We have another dead body here." She paused to listen to something he was saying, then continued. "Almost certainly connected, yes." She gave him our location and hung up.

"How are you feeling?" I asked Dot.

"This doesn't get any easier, does it? Seeing dead bodies, I mean," she replied. "I've no idea how Eddie deals with it day in and day out."

We stepped outside into the hallway, found the light switch, and lit cigarettes. My hand had a little tremor, which I allowed myself under the circumstances. We waited in silence for Eddie to arrive.

Twenty minutes later, we heard heavy footsteps on the stairs. Eddie's head appeared around the turn of the staircase, followed by a tall, skinny uniformed officer. Eddie looked towards Dot with concern written in the lines on his forehead, and then to me.

"Are you both okay?" he asked.

We told him yes.

He and the uniform stepped inside and crossed to the inner office. They stood and looked at the body for a few seconds, then took in the rest of the room.

"Call the coroner," Eddie told the uniform, who sat down at the reception desk, pulled on a glove, picked up the phone, and dialed a number.

Then Eddie came over to us. "So what do you think? Suicide again?" he said.

Apparently, one of the ways he dealt with corpses was with a dark sense of humor. I smiled weakly.

"Walk me through it," he said.

I let Dot tell the narrative, how we'd found the place dark, and that we'd touched both door handles, the phone, and the light switches.

"I'm not too worried about that," said Eddie. "We'll dust

of course, but I don't think we're going to find any prints. How does this play into the D'Amico story?"

Dot and I exchanged glances. "That's a bit complicated. Can we go somewhere and sit down?" I said.

Eddie stuck his head inside the door. "Martin, wait here for the coroner. If you need me, I'll be in Barney's taking statements."

Barney's, it turned out, was the bar on the corner. It was a bit more upscale than Jack's, which was to say that it didn't smell too much of sweat and stale beer, the seats weren't threadbare, there was no sawdust on the floor, and there were coasters on the bar counter. We took our drinks—beer for myself and Eddie, rye for Dot—over to a booth by the wall. Eddie pulled out his notebook and pencil.

"We're on the record for now," he said. "Why were you in Wetherby's office after hours?"

"I had an appointment with him, and Dot came along because I didn't want to be alone with him," I replied.

"Why not?"

"I was worried he might have gotten a bit handsy," I said. "He kind of creeped me out during a dinner meeting last night."

"You'd better tell it then," he said.

I told him the whole story from Wetherby coming to our office, my dinner with him and Logan, their plan to challenge the quitclaim and buy my half-interest in the property, and my decision to sell.

"I was wondering how they knew about the quitclaim and the suicide note too," I said. "Did you talk to anybody about the case?"

"Sure," replied Eddie. "We all do, even if it's just to complain about our bosses. I beefed about it in the bar, about it getting shut down as a suicide. A lot of the guys from the squad room were there, and some other guys from the precinct too. The case was closed, so I didn't think it would put somebody else in danger."

"Who had access to your report?"

"Almost anybody in the building could have pulled the jacket."

"Does this kind of leak happen a lot?" Dot asked.

"All the time, I'm afraid," replied Eddie. "Every studio, newsroom, and mobster in town has inside sources. Probably a lot of defense attorneys too. Most of the guys think of getting paid for inside info as a perk of the job. It doesn't exactly make my job easier."

"This crime scene looks like a set-up again, in my opinion," said Dot.

"Yeah," said Eddie. "It's supposed to look like a burglar went up there after hours expecting the place to be empty. When he surprised Wetherby, he killed him."

"And then he calmly went through his pockets for the safe keys, stepped over the bleeding body, and completed the burglary, all for whatever papers a lawyer has in his safe overnight," added Dot. "Unlikely."

"Agreed. But a detective who wasn't at the D'Amico scene could easily have read it that way. They probably didn't anticipate that I'd catch the call."

"If it's not a burglary, you're saying somebody targeted Wetherby," I said. "Presumably because of the deed. Seems like somebody doesn't want competition, and they're playing for keeps."

"A knife seems like a messy way to deal with somebody as harmless as Wetherby," mused Dot, her brow furrowed. "If they just wanted to kill him, they could have taken him somewhere else to do it, instead of leaving a crime scene potentially full of clues."

"Maybe that was a message to Logan. Maybe to warn him off his plan to discredit the quitclaim," I said.

"I don't want to scare you," said Eddie, "but I suspect that might be a message for you too, Joy. Whoever murdered Wetherby wants to make it clear that you shouldn't interfere in their deal."

I shuddered. I'd been wondering how much danger I was in. Now I knew.

"How could they know we'd be the ones to find the scene?" I said. "Nobody else knew about my appointment apart from his secretary."

"They didn't know. They'd assumed you'd read about it in the morning papers, along with everybody else in LA, and put two and two together. This is going to be front page material for the tabloids. As those guys say, 'if it bleeds, it leads'. Martin's probably already called his journalist contacts to send a photographer over before he calls the coroner."

"What now?" I asked. "Is somebody going to come after me to leave Lisa the only claimant?"

Eddie gave that some thought. "I don't think so. I don't think they would get rid of the lawyer so noisily and leave you out there. If they were coming for you, they wouldn't have given you a warning like this. As long as nobody pushes back on the quitclaim, there's no reason to harm you."

"For people who are trying to get hold of this property quietly, they sure are making a lot of noise," I said.

"True," said Eddie, "but remember, we're the only people who haven't closed the book on your father's supposed suicide. We're also the only people who see any connection between him and this murder."

"Whoever did this is definitely not going to give up on tracking down Helen," said Dot. "And when they find her, who knows what they'll do to get her to sign a document? And I'm worried about what they'd do to tidy up the loose ends once she has signed."

I sighed heavily. "We have no idea how Logan is going to react either. We don't know if he's a legit businessman or mobbed up. I hate to say this, but we need to make sure Helen knows she's in danger. If she doesn't give up this charade, she's going to get herself killed."

"Wait a second, who's Helen?" asked Eddie, his face screwed up in confusion.

"Oh, right," I said. "We didn't get a chance to tell you. Lisa D'Amico is an imposter. It turns out she's really a girl called Helen James, or so we think. She befriended Emma D'Amico and took her dead daughter's identity after Emma died. We assume she did all this because she saw a chance to claim the property."

"Jesus and Mary, this isn't a case, it's a maze," said Eddie. "How'd you figure that out?"

"That's the other thing you should know," said Dot. "Lisa, or Helen, ran out on Daubman, and he hired us to find her. We were digging into her background for leads."

"And you took Daubman on as a client?" said Eddie.

"What were you thinking?"

"Daubman seems kind of sketchy, but as far as we know, he could be completely innocent. At a stretch, he could even really be Helen's husband, as unlikely as that seems."

"Or he could be Tony D'Amico's killer," said Eddie.

"Or all of the above. We'd decided we'd try to find Lisa, hear her side of the story, and then figure out how to play it. Keeping Daubman close, and in the dark about our suspicions, seemed like the smartest move. It might be the best way of figuring out this whole mess."

"So wait. In that case, Helen James isn't entitled to any part of the property," said Eddie slowly. "If you can prove she's fake, the quitclaim doesn't matter either way, and the whole thing belongs to Joy, right?"

"Yeah, we had that thought too," I said, "but right now, our priority is keeping everybody safe, and for now, we don't even know who's a killer and who's potentially the next dead body. If whoever killed my father figures out that we're onto them, who knows what else they'll do to keep fake-Lisa's claim alive. So for the time being, we pretend to believe Lisa's story as far as anybody else is concerned."

"Who else knows about Helen James?" asked Eddie.

"For now, just the three of us," I said. "At least, as far as we know."

"I'm going to leave that out of my report," said Eddie. "It's probably safer for everybody that way."

He ordered another round. It wasn't our last that night.

Chapter Seventeen

I didn't sleep well that night, and finally gave up trying around five. After drinking some coffee and taking aspirin for my hangover, I decided I might as well get dressed and head to the office, so I could beat Dot there for once. If I didn't take the streetcar, it was a 30-minute walk, and I was up for it. The air was cool and clear and there was almost no traffic apart from the occasional cab cruising optimistically. I've always thought better moving, and I was still trying to untangle all the possible scenarios around this case. I couldn't figure out Daubman at all. He could be anything from distraught husband to hard-nosed killer, depending on what you wanted to believe. And I still had no idea why a scrubby bit of land squashed between two studio backlots was worth killing over.

I picked up a morning paper, and Eddie was right. Last night's bloody murder was all over the front page, with a lurid picture of the dead body.

I got to the office before seven, feeling very sure that we needed to find Helen if we wanted answers. Maybe she was only guilty of a clumsy attempt to steal a property deed, and if that was the case, she didn't deserve to become the next dead body in this business. Like it or not, we were going to have to try to run her to ground.

I put a fresh pot of coffee on around 8:45 a.m., and when Dot arrived at 8:55 a.m., I poured a cup for her. The bell on the outer door rang and I stepped out to see who it was. To my surprise, Eddie was standing there, a morning paper tucked under his arm.

"Hey, Joy. I dropped by to see how you and Dot were doing after last night. You don't see something like that too often." Ruefully, I reflected that Eddie probably saw it more often than anybody should have to.

"Come on through to the office," I told him. "I'll pour you a cup of cup of really bad coffee."

He followed me through the door and greeted Dot, who smiled and blushed bashfully.

He sniffed the coffee. "It's not great," he said, "But it still beats what they pour at the station."

The bell rang again. I left Dot and Eddie to their awkward flirting and went back out to the reception room. Standing in the middle of the floor, his face flushed, was somebody I had never expected to see again: Jerry Donaldson, my least favorite adulterer.

"You!" he shouted. "You cost me everything! My wife! My mistress! My… other mistress!"

"Mister, you're not getting anything you didn't earn," I told him, as calmly as I could manage. My heart was pounding.

He flexed and unflexed his fists, his face turning as red as the lobsters at Perino's.

"Let me tell you what I should do!" he yelled. "I should put a brick through that window of yours! Or maybe burn the place down! Or maybe I should just lay one on you right here and now!"

He stopped, and his face went from red to white like a curtain falling. I looked over my shoulder. Dot and Eddie were standing in the doorway to the inner office. Eddie had his coffee in one hand and his badge in the other.

"Could you repeat that last part?" said Dot. "I'm not sure the police detective got it all written down."

Donaldson stared, wide-eyed, frozen to the spot.

"Detective Ramirez, Los Angeles Police Department," Eddie said calmly. "Is there a problem here?"

"Uh… uh… no, not at all," sputtered Donaldson.

Eddie took four steps across the room and stood nose to nose with Donaldson, unblinking. "Good. Because if there ever is a problem for my friends, I will be all over you like that cheap suit of yours. In fact, you better pray you don't get so much as a jaywalking ticket, or the LAPD will be down on you like a ton of bricks."

Donaldson swallowed hard, stepped back, turned, and left without a backwards glance.

"Thanks, Eddie," I said. "I think we could've handled him, though."

"I know you could," replied Eddie, "But you shouldn't have to. Anyway, I have to run. I have a shift to work. Later."

Once he had gone, Dot and I settled down to our coffee and cigarettes. Compared to what we'd been through lately Donaldson was small fry, and I wasn't going to let him rattle me.

"Back to business," I said. "We need to get on with finding Helen, and then figure out how to play this so that nobody else ends up dead".

"I agree. There are far too many open questions right now."

We pulled out the map we'd marked up the previous day with the locations of our various Barrons. I sat back while Dot figured out the best route that meant the least amount of backtracking.

"There are three to the north of us, and three to the south, she said. "The north side is more accessible from the Red Line, so let's start with that."

All of the first three doors we knocked on had somebody home. We eliminated 'Sheila Baron' with one 'r' and one of the 'Sheila Barrons'. The third door was an unpretentious but well-cared for brick-built rowhouse, and it was the address of an 'S. Barron'. It was opened by an older woman, I guessed somewhere between a hard 40 and a well cared-for 50, obviously not a contemporary of Helen James. I asked anyway.

"Sheila Barron?" I said.

"I'm Sally Barron, are you perhaps looking for my daughter?"

"We might be. Did the two of you used to live over in Claremont?"

"Yes, but we moved out here a couple of years ago. And then Sheila moved again a few months back to share a place with some people her own age."

"Could you possibly give us that address?" I asked.

"That depends on why you're looking for her."

We hadn't rehearsed anything for this. I tried something that might work or might blow up completely.

"We have a message for her from her friend Helen James. Helen is in some trouble, and needs a little help."

Sally looked at us for several very long seconds before speaking. "Helen was always in trouble of some kind or another. She usually dragged Sheila into it too. When mothers said their child had gotten in with a bad crowd, it was Helen they were talking about. But I suppose Sheila is an adult now and needs to make her own decisions. Even the bad ones."

Dot pulled out the map and Sally located the address on it for us. It wasn't one of the addresses on our list. Without waiting for thanks or goodbyes, she closed the door on us.

"Lucky break," said Dot. "Maybe the first one in this whole case."

Thirty minutes later, we found ourselves in front of Barron's house. It was the left half of a modest two story duplex, stuccoed and tiled in the Spanish Revival style that had been popular in LA in the twenties. The lawn in front was little more than a postage stamp, and it looked like there was also a small yard in the back. The street was a lot nicer than some of the neighborhoods we'd been hanging out in lately, and Barron's house was no exception. It was no Hollywood mansion, but she was doing alright for herself for a girl from the slums.

"How do you want to play this?" I asked Dot.

"I'm going to take the back door in case she tries to run. Give me a minute before you knock."

She disappeared around the side of the building and I waited for her to get in position. I stepped up to the door and knocked, then stepped back. After a moment or two, the door opened to reveal a woman in her early twenties. She was slim, lightly made up, and neatly dressed in black slacks and a white button-down blouse. The clothes, like the house, looked to be in decent condition but nothing special.

"Miss Sheila Barron?" I said. "I'm a friend of Helen James. Is she here?"

Barron stared at me for a few seconds, sizing me up, I guessed. For a moment, I thought she was going to shut the door on me. Positioning herself so I couldn't easily step past her, she twisted and called inside: "Helen, you have a visitor!"

There was a scrape and a loud crash from inside, and then the sound of a door slamming. Barron jumped in alarm, turned, and scuttled inside. I followed her in. I took in the front room at a glance. There was a chintzy sofa just inside the door, and two armchairs that matched each other but not the sofa. Across the room, there was a small wooden dining table with four chairs around it, one of them sprawled on the floor, and just behind it, there was a large serving hatch that opened into a modest kitchen. It was the first place I'd been in for a while that had more than a kitchenette. I guessed the house might be shared by three or four girls. Next to the table, a door to the back part of the house stood ajar. I was halfway across the room to it when it opened wider. Helen came through it squirming, and right behind her, Dot with her hand clamped around Helen's upper arm, pushing her along.

"Hello, Helen," I said. She sagged. I suspected only Dot's grip was keeping her upright.

"Listen," said Dot, "We're trying to help you. You've dug yourself into a lot of trouble."

"And trust us," I added, "We're no friends of Daubman."

Barron looked from Dot to myself and back again. "Who are you people, and what is going on here?" she demanded. "If you're trouble for Helen, you'll have to deal with me too."

"Can we sit down and talk?" I said to Barron. "It will become a lot clearer. And if our story doesn't ring true to you, we'll leave quietly and neither one of you will see us again. I promise."

Barron looked at us for a moment, chewing her lip and spoiling her perfect lipstick. Then she looked to Helen for some sort of direction. Helen just nodded.

Barron sighed. "Very well," she said. "Is this going to be brief, or should I make coffee and settle in for the long run?"

"Probably not brief," said Dot.

Sheila went over to the kitchen and started fussing with coffee and hot water, watching and listening through the hatch. Dot set Helen down in the middle of the sofa and sat next to her. I took the armchair at the other end of the sofa. If Helen decided to make another run for it, Dot would have the front door covered and I would have the back.

"In case it's not obvious, we tracked you down because we've figured out that you're not Lisa D'Amico," I said. "And we don't think you're married to Daubman either, not even under a false name, but tell me if I'm wrong. You're Helen James, a girl who helped out Emma D'Amico, and you stayed with her right up until her death. Accurate so far?"

Helen nodded miserably. Barron looked unsurprised.

"Sheila, do we need to spell any of that out for you?" I called through to the kitchen.

"No," she called back. "Helen brought me up to speed on that part when she turned up here."

I wondered what version of events Helen had told, but no matter.

"When Emma died and you were sorting out her possessions, is that when you found the deed and got the idea?"

Helen shook her head. "No, I'd known about the deed for a long time. Emma often talked about it, like she was keeping it for when Tony came back one day. It was crazy, but nothing could convince her he was gone for good. I knew about little Lisa too, and when I found her birth certificate, that's when I got the idea. After all, the deed was just sitting there unclaimed. Tony certainly didn't deserve it back, not after abandoning Emma like that, and Emma doesn't have any other family. And I was the one who had cared for Emma. I surely earned something for my trouble. Emma would have wanted it that way."

I didn't know whether I wanted to swallow that, but I didn't interrupt.

"So I figured I could pose as the next-of-kin, inherit the property, and cash in," she continued. "Nobody would get hurt, and otherwise, it would have just gone to the state. I had no idea it was going to get so rough."

"So you came to us to do the search for Tony, never expecting we'd find him."

"Yes," said Lisa. "Daubman said he wouldn't get involved with that. He said it might attract attention if he suddenly started looking for Tony D'Amico himself. It had to be done at arm's length or not at all. He told me to bring him a clean title to the property in my name, or forget it."

Barron came in with coffee and handed it around. Helen blew on hers and took a deep swallow.

"Does he know you're not really Lisa D'Amico?"

"No. He suspected there's something hinky, but he didn't know just why I didn't want anybody looking too closely at the deal."

"How did you get connected with Daubman anyway?" Dot asked.

"A friend of mine had sometimes done work for him, when Daubman needed to avoid getting his own hands dirty. I have some rough friends. I asked him to make the introduction after I discovered the lot was next to Mammoth's backlot and figured it might be worth something to them."

"And then we ruined everything when we found Tony alive," I said.

"Yes, you did," replied Helen. She looked completely miserable.

"How much did you know about his killing?" I asked.

"I didn't want anything to do with it, but Daubman threatened me. He said I could go to jail for fraud for trying to sell him a deed that didn't belong to me. I didn't know if that was true, but I was worried that he'd guessed something, so I went along with it. He told me all I had to do was knock on the door loud enough for the neighbors to hear, then call the police and pretend I'd heard a crash inside. It was my idea to call you two. I thought it would make my story better if you backed me up on how I found Tony."

Dot nodded. That made sense. Somebody less observant than Dot would probably have confirmed her version of events.

"Is that when you began to be scared of Daubman?" I asked.

"Yes. I started to wonder if he'd get rid of me too, once he had the deed in his possession. You know, to cover his trail."

"But you stayed for a few more days."

"Yes. I was scared to run and scared to stay. But I reckoned I was safe as long as I hadn't signed the deed over to him."

"What made you finally decide to run out on him?"

"Another man approached me, offering more money than Daubman was promising. He also said he could sink my sole claim to the property if I didn't do business with him."

"Was he a greasy little lawyer called Wetherby?" I asked.

"That's him. You two are good. Anyway, I told him no because I was afraid to cross Daubman. I told Daubman all about Wetherby that night, and said I should get more money. I didn't even ask for as much as Wetherby offered, I just wanted a better deal. Daubman said he'd take care of Wetherby, but I wasn't getting any more money. It turned into a big argument, and that's when I finally got scared enough to leave."

Interesting. Either Daubman was definitely a killer, or Helen was a prolific liar. Or maybe both.

"Somebody certainly took care of Wetherby," I said.

"What do you mean?"

"You haven't seen a morning paper? Somebody went to Wetherby's office last night and killed him. Cut his throat."

Helen looked shocked. For once, it might have been genuine.

"You have to realize by now, you're in danger as long as Daubman thinks you're Lisa," I said. "The only way you get out from under is by confessing to Daubman."

Helen looked ready to cry, maybe even for real this time. "Girls like me never catch a break, do they?"

Sheila came over, put her arm around Helen, and gave her

a squeeze, before going back to her seat. She seemed completely unfazed by the whole saga. Maybe she'd already heard most of it. Maybe scrapes like this were a habit for Helen.

"What happens now?" said Helen.

"First, we have to get you somewhere safe," said Dot. "It took us half a day to find this place, so I don't expect it to take Daubman's people much longer. They might even be tailing us."

"I know a place that'll work for a couple of days," I said. "That should be long enough to figure out how to straighten out Daubman."

Helen raised her eyebrows in surprise. "You'd do that for me?"

"Don't mistake this for kindness," I said. "I want this whole business over with and you gone from my life without anybody else getting killed. Not even you. I don't like you one bit, but you don't deserve to die over some dumb con gone south."

Helen sighed heavily. "I'll pack my things," she said. She got up from the sofa and headed for the stairs.

"You're not going to do something stupid like jump out a window, are you?" said Dot. "We're trying to keep you alive here."

"They're right, Helen," said Sheila. "Do something smart for once."

"Don't worry," said Helen. "I'm done running. I just want this to be over." She disappeared upstairs.

Dot raised her eyebrows at me. "I think I'll wait out back, just in case," she said.

"Probably wise," said Sheila as Helen disappeared upstairs. "Knowing Helen, she's never too far away from making a bad choice."

We waited quietly for about 10 minutes until Helen came downstairs, her little yellow suitcase in hand. Sheila went out back and called Dot inside. Dot and I thanked Sheila and shook her hand.

She gave Helen a long hug. "Be careful, please," she said to Helen. And to us, said, "Try to keep her out of trouble for 15 minutes."

We filed out the front door and headed towards the Red Line stop, Helen walking between the two of us. We'd gone half a block when a big green sedan pulled up to the curb alongside us. As we passed, the rear suicide door opened and a large man in a dark suit stepped out behind us.

"Excuse me, Lisa?" he said.

She stopped and turned. Without warning, he wrapped an arm around her and lifted her off her feet. She started kicking and screaming, and tried to swing her bag at him, but her arms were pinned. I grabbed one of his arms. He tried to shake me off without letting go of Helen, but I clung on doggedly. Dot grabbed his other arm and kicked his ankles.

The front door of the car opened and another man got out, tall and wiry. He peeled me off the first man's arm and tossed me hard to the ground. I tumbled over twice and sat up dazed, just in time to see him drag Dot off and throw her against a wall. She went down too.

The big man wrangled Helen into the back of the car like an uncooperative sack of laundry, and the wiry one slammed the door shut behind him. He jumped in the front and the car peeled away, leaving only rubber and exhaust behind.

Helen's little yellow suitcase lay forlornly on the sidewalk, open. Its pathetic few contents had spilled out.

Chapter Eighteen

We were sat in Café del Sol with Eddie, taking in the comforting aroma of café de olla. Dot had scrapes on her hands, elbows, and knees, and holes in her stockings. I had bruises in places that didn't show. There are advantages to wearing a leather flight jacket and gabardine slacks. Both of us were shaken, but settling down. Eddie had his notebook out.

"Did you get a look at the two guys?" he asked.

I shook my head. "It was over pretty damn quick. One was big and one was wiry, and that's about all I can tell you."

"I don't have anything more than that," said Dot. "Sorry."

"What about the car?" asked Eddie.

"Dark green Chrysler Royale, '38," said Dot promptly.

"That's very specific," said Eddie, his eyebrows raised.

"The '38 had a distinctive grille compared to the '37, and the '39 was a significant restyling."

"Okay then. I don't suppose you got the license plate?"

Dot recited it for him.

"So you got the make, model, year, and plate, but not the guys' faces?"

"Sorry," said Dot, "I'm just not good at faces."

Eddie shook his head. "I'll check out who it's registered to, but it's a fair bet that it's stolen. If they're smart, they already ditched the car," said Eddie. "Fortunately for us, these people are often not very smart. Maybe we'll get lucky."

We took our time finishing our coffee and headed back to the office.

Outside our door, a black coupe was parked with its

motor idling. Usually I wouldn't pay any attention, but after the earlier ambush, my hackles were raised. I looked inside, and was surprised to see Logan. He raised his hand in the same two-fingered salute I'd seen at Perino's, opened the door, and stepped out.

"Can we talk inside?" he asked.

Dot opened the door and led us through to the back. She put hot water on for coffee. I sat behind my desk and Logan sat across from me. He didn't wait for an invitation. He put his hands palm-down on my desk and splayed his spider-leg fingers. I shivered. As before, the image of them encircling a neck came to mind.

"I expect you've heard the sad news about Wetherby?" he asked. "It's in all the morning papers."

I didn't bother to tell him we'd seen it for ourselves in person. He didn't seem too broken up about it.

"I don't get the point of it," said Dot, playing dumb. "Surely you can get another lawyer. It's simple contract work."

"Wetherby's death was a warning," said Logan. "Somebody is telling us to stay away from this business. All of us."

"So what happens now?" I asked. "Are you out?"

"We're no longer trying to buy out your interest. We've decided to pursue an alternative business strategy," said Logan.

I waited to see if he would elaborate. Dot set coffee in front of us. I picked mine up and sipped it. Nothing was forthcoming.

"Does this alternative strategy involve snatching people

off the street in broad daylight?" I finally asked.

He flinched. It was very brief, but I caught it.

"Are you going to tell us why this property is worth a murder and a kidnapping?" asked Dot. I noted how she cleverly avoided letting on that we knew Tony's death was also a murder. First rule of intelligence.

"I'm not at liberty to say. All I can tell you is that it would be safest for the both of you to drop the matter entirely. It's only going to get rougher from here on in," replied Logan. "I'd forget anything you've heard about the quitclaim."

He stood up. His coffee was untouched.

"I'll see myself out," he said.

We waited until we had heard the front door ring him out.

Dot topped off my coffee. "How are you feeling?" she asked.

"Jerked around," I replied. I lit a Lucky Strike. "What do you think Logan's play is?"

"It sounds like he's given up on invalidating the quitclaim and buying the two halves from you and Helen, or Lisa, as he still thinks she is. I think he'll hold her until she can be persuaded to sell to his people."

"'Persuaded'?"

"Do I have to spell it out? It won't be good."

"I don't want to think what her life will be worth once he has her signature," I said.

The phone rang. We both picked up. It was Eddie.

"Good timing, ace. I was just about to call you. Do you have some good news for us?"

"Not really," said Eddie. "Highway Patrol says the car had been reported stolen a few hours earlier. It hasn't turned up yet and they probably ditched it somewhere, but you never know. What's your news?"

"Logan came here to warn us off. His offer to me is off the table. His face confessed to grabbing Helen, but he didn't say it in so many words."

"I'll work my contacts to see if anybody knows who Logan is, but it's a slim chance. We don't even have a first name for him."

"I do have Logan's license plate though," said Dot.

"Of course you do," I said.

Dot gave the number to Eddie, who promised to chase it down. I hoped it wouldn't be a dead end like the last one. We hung up.

"Are we going to back off?" Dot asked.

"Not willingly," I replied. "I don't take well to being threatened. But unless you have another idea, we're out of leads."

"We should call Daubman and let him know what's happened, I suppose," said Dot. "Or at least, some version of it."

I didn't like it, but I didn't have anything better. And sooner or later, we were going to have to tell Daubman we had no idea where Helen now was.

Chapter Nineteen

The weekend came and went. Life returned to something like its normal rhythms, although worries about Helen still lurked at the back of my head and my frustration with the whole business wasn't going away either. Dot was visibly irritated by all the loose threads the case had left dangling. Eddie had no news for us on finding Logan, nor identifying Wetherby's killer. We were completely stymied.

I was drinking coffee and going over events in my head, trying to think of ways we might track down Helen, when the morning mail brought us an unexpected gift. It was a postcard, addressed to me. On the front was a picture of the neon signs of Las Vegas, and on the back, a brief message written in Helen's childish print:

Dear Sis,

Wish you were here! This town is amazing. If you can believe it, they have brothels! Tell Alex I miss him.

Love, Lisa

It was postmarked Saturday in Las Vegas. I showed it to Dot.

"What do you make of that?" asked Dot.

"'Wish you were here'? It's a cry for help," I said. "Calling me 'Sis' out of nowhere is also a big warning flag."

"Yes, it's not the toughest code I've ever come across. I assume she's being held there by whoever snatched her, but she managed to get a message out. For whatever reason, she had to make it sound innocuous. And she wants to make up with Daubman, presumably because it's better than her current situation. I don't get the reference to brothels, though."

"There are supposedly no brothels in Las Vegas these days. The army had them shut down in '42 when they built a base there. Apparently, they caused a lot of trouble. The city wasn't happy about it, but I guess they decided that an army base was more valuable."

"You've been to Las Vegas?"

"I delivered a B-17 there one time. It's an ugly, low-rent dump in the middle of a desert, so it's perfect for an artillery target practice base."

"So she's telling us she's being held in an unlicensed brothel somewhere in town. I assume that just because they're illegal, it doesn't mean there aren't a few still quietly operating. At least that narrows down the search a little."

I sat and fumed. "Damn it, I don't think we can just abandon her. If she's reaching out to us, she obviously doesn't have anybody else."

"True, but we can't just drive to Las Vegas and run around town asking people if they know of any illegal brothels."

"Yeah. I heard the whole town is mobbed up. We're way out of our depth. We need help from somebody who knows their way around," I said. "I hate to say it, but I think we're going to have to ask Daubman for help, while pretending we don't think he probably killed my father. Once we know what the score is with Helen, we can figure out our next move."

"Is that smart? Do we believe that Daubman didn't kill Wetherby?"

"At this point, I would believe it, but I don't know if we have much of a choice. We don't have to trust him, but we do at least have to pretend to trust him. Daubman has resources, and he might even know who Logan is. As for Helen, would being found by Daubman be worse than being held by Logan? After all, Helen seems to be signaling that we should reach out to him."

Dot gave that some thought. "Well, objectively speaking, we still don't know for sure that he's actually done anything criminal. We only have Helen's word for that," she said.

"And Helen lies like a rug," I shot back.

I picked up the phone and called Daubman's office. His secretary picked up on the third ring, and transferred me over to him.

"Lisa is in Las Vegas, and we think somebody is holding her there against her will," I told him. "We need a car. And any contacts you have there."

"I can do better than that," said Daubman. "Can you meet me at the Lockheed Air Terminal, say at two? Look for the sign saying General Aviation. And pack a bag for a couple of days."

I hung up.

"Sounds like Daubman is going to spring for plane tickets," I told Dot, not even trying to hide the surprise in my voice.

We met Daubman on time, and he handed us passes on lanyards. "You'll need these," he said. He was already wearing one himself.

"You're coming with us?" said Dot.

"Of course. It sounds like Lisa is in physical danger. And you're going to need me to navigate that town," replied Daubman.

I was starting to realize that we really had no idea what we were walking into. And I was starting to worry about walking into it with Daubman.

Daubman led us past a uniformed guard who took a cursory look at our passes. Then we went through a pair of swinging doors into a crude waiting area with a concrete floor and cheap wooden bench seats. I put my hand on Daubman's elbow and tugged on him to stop.

"I need to say something," I told him. "If we're going to take this flight with you, we need some honesty."

"What do you mean?" he said.

"You're not really married to Lisa, are you?"

Dot looked at me with her eyebrows arched. We hadn't discussed this, and it broke her rule about not sharing intelligence you didn't have to. But I needed to see if he would level with us.

Daubman paused for several long seconds. "No," he finally said.

"Then you'd better tell us what your interest is. And it had better be more than 'jilted lover' or 'she took my favorite watch'."

He paused again, gathering his thoughts. Or maybe he was deciding how much of the truth to tell us.

"Lisa brought a business proposal to me that's important to Mammoth. It's nothing illegal, but it's essential that we don't attract attention and alert other bidders. She had nowhere to stay, so I set her up in the hotel like she was a girlfriend. It also gave us a cover story if anybody saw us meeting.

"When she tried to go back on our deal and demand more money, we argued, and that's when she ran out on me. I thought she would get back in contact, and when she didn't, I asked you to find her so we could re-negotiate, because I still need that deal. And I genuinely did worry that she might have gotten herself in trouble over it. But now, she's definitely in danger, and I feel responsible for that."

I let that hang for a few seconds before replying. "Okay, that story I mostly believe. I don't think it's the whole truth, but it'll do for now. We can talk about the rest when Lisa is safely back in LA."

"Since we're being transparent with each other, there's something I also need to ask," said Daubman. "Lisa's real name is D'Amico. That seems like quite a coincidence."

I glanced at Dot. She was impressively impassive.

"It's a common enough name for Italian Americans," I shrugged. "It would be a surprise to me if we're related." Technically, all of that was true, and it seemed like an effective way of sidestepping Daubman's question. I had no idea whether Daubman bought it. For the moment, we both seemed to have decided to pretend we believed each other.

We went on through the waiting area and out the doors on the far side, where a silver-skinned two-engined airplane was idling on the tarmac.

"Oh, cool!" I exclaimed. "A C-47!"

Dot looked at me quizzically.

"It's a military version of the DC-3," I explained. Dot still looked blank. "They built thousands of them during the war, and now they're selling off the surplus planes for civilian use. They're really tough birds, and they say they're a real pleasure to fly."

We climbed the steps to the door behind the wing. Inside,

the cabin had been converted from its original troop carrier configuration to four groups of upholstered benches around wooden tables. A smiling uniformed stewardess greeted us and stowed our bags. The three of us sat around one of the tables.

"How did you wrangle this?" I asked Daubman.

"It belongs to Mammoth," he replied. "We use it for lots of things, like taking stars out to location shoots, especially in the desert, or junkets to Las Vegas or Reno, so people can blow off steam out of sight of the Hollywood press. The executives use it for breaks in Palm Springs. And occasionally, somebody needs to leave town discreetly. I have the option to use it when I need it for work. And as I just confessed inside, strictly speaking, this is work."

I looked across at Dot. She was pale, and very obviously anxious.

"You okay?" I asked.

"First time in a plane," she said. I could hear the tautness in her voice.

"Really? How did you get out to D.C. when you worked for the army?"

"Buses. Long ride."

"You'll be fine," I told her. "Just think of it as a Greyhound, except it's thousands of feet in the air." As I said that, I realized it probably wasn't as reassuring as I'd intended.

"How about you?" said Daubman. "Not your first time, I take it."

"First time when I couldn't see where I was going," I replied.

"You're a flier? Go on up front, see if they'll let you sit up there."

I got up and made my way forward, knocked on the open cockpit door, and waited to be asked in.

"Oh, hi," said the pilot. "I'm Jerry and this is Andy." He indicated his co-pilot.

"Joy. Do you mind if I join you?" I asked. "I'm more used to being up front than in back."

"You fly?" said Jerry. "Great. Take the navigator seat. We're just finishing up pre-flight checks and talking to the tower, so we're going to ignore you until we're at altitude."

"Thanks," I said. I sat down and buckled in. I'd seen inside a number of C-47s during the war—it was hard to find a military base that didn't have a couple sitting on the tarmac—but I'd never flown one. In military configuration, the C-47 had as many as four crew, with seats for a radio operator and a navigator as well as the two pilots. In civilian use, it only required the pilots and they handled the other duties between themselves. From what I'd heard, it could even be flown single-handed in a pinch. I listened to the familiar back and forth with the tower as we taxied out, and kept to myself until we reached 10,000 feet. The plane was capable of much higher altitude, but we'd make good speed at this height.

Andy twisted around. "You want to sit in for a bit?" he asked. "We're very casual when nobody's watching."

"Absolutely!" I said.

He got up and we swapped seats.

"Any chance I could take the controls?" I asked Jerry.

He looked skeptical. "Have you flown anything this size

before?"

"Well, I'm used to having two more engines than this, but I think I'll manage," I smiled.

Jerry laughed. "Ferry pilot?" he asked.

"Yep."

"What did you fly?"

"B-17s," I said, taking the yoke.

"You'll find this a whole lot lighter. You want to make some S-curves, see how she handles?"

"For sure," I said. I made a gentle turn to port, then back to starboard, then straight and level, then did the same the other way. Jerry watched me closely the whole time.

I'd missed this so much. If I had the money to get it off the ground, I would start an air charter business and fly full-time.

"Really nice," I said. "I appreciate it, but I'm going to give you your ship back now. I need to see how my friend Dot is getting on back there."

Andy took his seat back. "Come on up again later if you like," he said. "You're much prettier company than Jerry here."

"And you're a better flier than Andy," retorted Jerry.

When I reached the back, Dot was looking a lot less anxious. Apparently, she'd had some nausea during the climb, but was feeling better now that we were straight and level. I hoped my brief turn at the controls hadn't bothered her. The rye that the stewardess had served her was helping too. Apparently, they had a well-stocked bar on board, so I asked for a Scotch.

"We've got about an hour and half before we start down,"

said Daubman. "I'm going to take a nap." He moved to one of the other tables, laid himself out on the bench, and was asleep in minutes. Dot retrieved a book from her suitcase. I went forward to enjoy the feeling of flying again.

We picked up a moderate tailwind and ninety minutes later we were on the ground at Alamo Field, on the south side of town. We parked near a cluster of hangers, some of them occupied by private planes like ours as well as single-engine hobbyists. Other planes sat out on the tarmac. We waited while steps were brought up to the door, then made our way down to the tarmac, across to the single story, flat-roofed stucco building that served as a terminal, and out the other side where a chauffeur and a limo were waiting for us. Apparently, Daubman had called ahead. The driver was a white man in his fifties with graying hair peeking out from under his chauffeur's cap. He had a look that said this wasn't his dream job, but it was better than working construction, tending bar, or dealing blackjack, which were probably the other major options in this town. I disliked being in the back of a car almost as much as I disliked being in the back of a plane, but I didn't make a fuss.

The limo took us down Fremont Street, lined with casinos and showhouses, most of them looking like something out of a Western movie, which is to say, these were not classy joints. Windows were grimy with desert sand, and paint was fading and peeling under the harsh sun. The whole place looked every bit as sketchy as I remembered it from '43, and I wondered why anybody from Hollywood would come out here. Then we headed out of town a little way, where I hadn't been before, and things got a lot more interesting. There were two much classier looking hotels out here, and a third one going up.

"The El Rancho and the Last Frontier are much more upscale than Fremont Street," said Daubman. "This is where we bring our people to stay and play. But the Flamingo, that's going to be something else entirely. It'll be a proper big city casino and luxury hotel with big-name entertainers. At least, that's Bugsy's plan."

"Bugsy?" said Dot.

"Bugsy Siegel," I explained. "He's a major figure with the New York Families."

"That's right," said Daubman. "And he thinks Las Vegas can be something seriously high-end with the right investment. It's a huge gamble."

We pulled up in front of the Last Frontier.

"This is where we're staying. It's also where Bugsy is holding court, and where I'm going to pay my respects before we make any moves in his town."

"What about us?" I asked.

"You'll have to amuse yourselves for a while. Bugsy can be unpredictable, especially with women."

I didn't like it, but apparently, we didn't have much say in the matter. Dot and I left our bags with the driver and a bell boy, and took a walk over to the bar via the casino. The floor was mostly empty at this time of day, just a couple of desultory tables of blackjack and craps. The carpets were thick, the veneers were thin, and the smiles on the croupiers were strained. Over against the far wall, a line of one armed bandits were flashing their lights and ringing their bells desperately seeking attention, paper-thin glitz to create an illusion of fun for people lonely enough to gamble alone. The word for it all was 'gaudy', and I quickly found the whole spectacle depressing. Maybe it came alive at night, but this seemed like a sad way to spend an afternoon.

Daubman found us 30 minutes later at the hotel bar. Dot was drinking Coke and I was stretching out a beer and trying to pick up my mood.

"Did you try the tables?" he asked.

"No," I answered listlessly. "Dot is too smart to gamble, and I'm too broke. Whoever this place is designed for, it's not people like us."

He looked disappointed, almost personally hurt, but tried to recover. "Good news," he told us. "Bugsy is having his people ask around if anybody has seen Lisa. He says he knows nothing about her being taken, and he's not at all keen on anything unsanctioned happening on his turf. And he's okayed us to ask our own questions in town, provided we do it quietly and don't make trouble."

"And if we find her?" I asked.

"Provided it's not one of Bugsy's people holding her, we're free to deal with it ourselves, and he doesn't want to know about it. Again, provided it's quiet. If it is one of his boys, we're to report back and he'll handle it."

I wasn't sure I liked the sound of any of that, but it was what we had, and we would have to make the most of it.

"If you're rested, we can start right away," added Daubman.

I didn't know if rested was the right word. I felt simultaneously tired yet restless and anxious. But it was better than spending the rest of the afternoon at the casino bar.

We grabbed our purses, followed Daubman out to the curb, and waited for the driver to bring the limo around. I squinted in the sunlight. Daubman slipped sunglasses on, and I handed Dot my Ray-Ban Aviators. I could really use them myself, but the way Dot's blue eyes were watering in the glare, she clearly needed them more than me.

"Drop us at Fremont Street, then bring the limo back here and knock off for the day. We'll get a cab back when we're done," Daubman told the driver.

The driver dropped us at the west end of the street, in front of the train depot. There were at least a couple of dozen casinos, hotels, restaurants, and bars on each side of the street. After that the street disappeared into dust and heat haze. Nearest to us were the Overland Hotel on the left and the Sal Sagev Hotel on the right. Further down I could see signs for the Pioneer, the El Cortez, the Frontier Club, the Hotel Apache, and the Monte Carlo. I suspected the latter was a little less glamorous than its more famous namesake. Fremont Street had grown since I was last here a few years back, and to my surprise, I realized I was eager to see the neon lit up at night.

"Let's start at the Overland and work our way up the left, then back down the right. You two keep eyes and ears open, and let me do the talking," said Daubman. It promised to be a long and tedious afternoon, but then again, a lot of detective work was like that.

We walked into the Overland's bar. It was a rough looking place, rougher even than Jack's back in LA. I wasn't sure whether the sawdust on the floor was a nod to the Western theme, or because it really was a spit and sawdust kind of joint. I could see the relative appeal of a place like the Last Frontier, which at least was clean and probably reasonably honest. Dot and I hung back while Daubman approached the barman. A brief conversation ended with a shake of the head from the latter. Daubman wrote something down for him, presumably our contact details, then returned to us.

"He's seen nothing, but he promised to ask the other staff when they change over for the evening shift. We should also check with the hotel desk."

That conversation proved just as fruitless. Stepping outside from the darkness of the bar, the blazing sun was blinding. My eyes started to water. Shading our eyes with our hands as best we could, we walked a few feet to the café next door. Instead of sawdust on the floor, it had cheap linoleum, covered with scuff marks from years of shoes and boots. It was no better than the kind of places I used to seek out in LA when I was short on cash, but this one was a lot pricier. Again, Daubman got nothing.

We continued in this fashion to a third, a fourth, a sixth place, and we had made our way only a fraction of the way up the street. I was tired, sweaty, thirsty, and my feet ached. The sidewalk was too hot and every surface radiated heat. My eyes hurt from the alternating unfiltered sunlight and dark interiors. I could feel a headache coming on. Dot looked worse than I felt. Even the immaculate Daubman was starting to look creased and weathered. We stepped into one more place, a bar that looked slightly less unattractive than its predecessors. At least the floor was clear of sawdust.

"Who thought it was a good idea to build a resort in the middle of the desert?" grumbled Dot. "This whole place should have been left to the sands once the Boulder dam was finished."

"Let's get a drink and reassess," I said. "We could do this all day and get nowhere."

Daubman ordered himself a Scotch and water, and a beer for me. Dot asked for her usual straight rye.

"Have a glass of water with that," I told her. "You're dehydrated, and straight alcohol will make it worse."

She nodded her agreement.

We sat around a scratched and dented table that looked like it had been refinished a few times simply by applying one more layer of varnish over the existing ones. We sipped our drinks in silence, trying to regain some energy.

Daubman spoke first. "What's the deal, Joy?" He sounded a little tetchy, which was understandable.

"Just look at the number of places on this street alone, and that's not even counting other streets like Block 16," I said. "Every hotel has a casino and every casino has a bar. Are we going to ask every barman and every croupier in town, and then come back for the night shift? We don't know if she is even allowed out to drink or gamble. We might be completely wasting our time in bars and casinos. And nobody is going to admit to us they have an illegal brothel upstairs."

"That's only half of it," said Dot. "This whole town is transient. Visitors are coming and going every day, and I suspect that the staff turnover is huge too. Nobody is paying enough attention to anybody else to remember who they saw. The people working here probably don't remember any face more than 30 seconds after they've taken their money."

"We've got more chance of just bumping into her in the

street," I added. "She might even not still be here, if her kidnapper twigged to what the postcard meant. Maybe this whole trip out here was a mistake. Maybe we got carried away."

Daubman looked deeply unhappy. "Yeah, perhaps it was. But I don't know what else we can do. Do we just sit around and wait for word from Siegel's people? I can't hang around here for days, I have business back in LA."

"You're not the only one," I said.

"But I also can't just abandon Lisa," said Daubman listlessly.

"That too," I agreed.

"Siegel's people have a lot more eyes and ears and feet than we do. If we're going to wait for word from Siegel, maybe we should do our waiting back in LA," said Dot. "If you're willing to make the plane available again, we can be back here in two hours if anything comes up."

All three of us sat quietly, sipping the dregs of our drinks.

"How about this?" said Daubman. "Let's get a taxi back to the Last Frontier for now. We'll stay overnight and see if anything turns up. If not, we'll head back to LA in the morning and wait for a call."

"Okay, that sounds reasonable," said Dot.

Daubman settled the tab and we walked slowly down to the west end of Fremont Street, the sun in our eyes as it started to head for the horizon. We quickly found a cab. I told the driver I was a cabbie too and he let me ride up front, while Dot and Daubman rode in the back seat. All the windows were open which at least created a breeze, even if it was a hot and dusty one.

The cab dropped us in front of the hotel and Daubman paid off the driver. We stepped inside the air conditioned lobby and I felt my body temperature drop immediately. The sweat that was beading on my back turned icy cold. I shivered. It was the best I had felt in hours.

"Somebody should put air conditioning in cars," I said.

"Packard tried it in 1939," said Dot. "It was expensive, it took up most of the trunk, and it was hopelessly unreliable. They discontinued it after a year." I should have known better than to talk about cars in front of Dot.

Refreshed by the cold air, I felt like I could once again contemplate the future. "What do we want to do with our evening in Las Vegas?" I asked.

"I brought a book that I'd like to finish," said Dot.

"No, come on," I replied. "We should do something more fun while we're here. Take our minds off the waiting."

"They have an amazing chorus line in the show here," said Daubman. "You really should see it at least once."

Dot didn't look too excited, but I nudged her. "Do something a little out of the ordinary," I told her.

"Very well," she said. "But if I hate it, I'm leaving, no questions asked, no criticism tomorrow."

"Fair enough," I replied.

"Let's meet back here for dinner at seven, and see the show at eight," said Daubman. "Now, I have to go and make some calls. Like I said, business didn't stop just because I came out here."

Dot and I went up to the room we were sharing.

"What's your plan?" she asked.

"I'm going to take a nap, then shower before dinner.

You?"

"I'm going to shower right now. I feel filthy. My whole skin is itchy, and I can't stand it a minute longer. I'll try not to wake you with the noise."

"No chance," I said. I kicked off my shoes, lay down on the bed, and was asleep before she had her clothes off.

I woke up at about five and took my shower. By the time I was done and wearing clean clothes, I felt a lot better.

"Listen," I said, "something's been bothering me since we got here, and I finally figured out what it is."

Dot put down the book she'd been reading. "Go ahead," she said.

"How does a man like Daubman have such an in with the mob? I mean, I understand he comes to Las Vegas a lot to mind his stars, and he probably has some contacts to keep them out of trouble, but a personal meeting with Bugsy Siegel himself? That's some high level stuff."

"Is it?" asked Dot. "I don't really know much about those guys."

"I wish we knew more about him. It's starting to feel important."

"You're not going to like this, but I do have one thought."

"Go ahead," I said cautiously.

"Maybe Accardo knows something."

I sat up straight and stiff. Accardo was a mobster that we'd run into while we were working our very first case together. It was how we had met. And the last time I'd seen him, I'd been his hostage. "Are you going to call?" I said.

"I think I tried his patience last time," replied Dot. By an elaborate sequence of events, a book of blackmail material that was potentially damaging to Accardo had fallen into Dot's hands. It was keeping us safe from him. But it was a brittle standoff at best.

"It didn't exactly go well for me either," I reminded her. "And you seem to be able to talk to him in terms he understands."

We looked at each other for a long ten seconds.

"I suppose you're right," she finally said. "But if he won't talk to me, you'll have to try."

Dot had the number memorized, because her brain works like that. She dialed the operator and asked her to connect her long-distance. I put my ear up against the receiver to listen in as best I could. The line rang a couple of times before a woman's voice came on.

"Yeah?" the voice said harshly.

"It's Dot Stone. Would you ask Mr. Accardo if he can come to the phone?"

There was some noise on the line, then silence, then footsteps.

"Miss Stone, this is a surprise," said Accardo flatly. I suddenly felt very cold. The time I'd spent as his prisoner all came back to me. I tried to pull myself together.

"Joy D'Amico is here with me. I'll come straight out with it. We're calling to ask a favor."

"I hope you don't think you can squeeze more juice out of our existing arrangement," said Accardo. "That would make me very unhappy."

I noticed how careful he was not to say anything that might incriminate himself. Accardo talked as if he assumed his calls were always being tapped. And on a long-distance call, it was very much possible the operator was still listening in.

"Absolutely not," Dot said. "That arrangement was final and we abide by it." The arrangement being that Accardo left us alone, and the material damaging to his business did not come out.

"Okay, good. So why would I do you a favor?" he asked.

"Because then we would owe you a favor, and I think you're the kind of man who likes to be owed favors."

"What kind of favor could people like you offer to somebody like me?" he said scornfully.

Dot was prepared for that. "Have you ever suspected that your girlfriend is not entirely faithful to you? Or that one of your business managers is not being completely forthcoming about revenues? We're very good at finding out that kind of thing, and we're very discreet."

I didn't feel great about us being in his debt, even though Dot was being very clear about the kind of things we might do to settle up. There was no hiding the fact that Accardo was a mobster who routinely shook people down. But he liked to think of himself as a rational businessman first and foremost, just one whose businesses were mostly illegal and often involved extortion. As he saw it, he resorted to as little violence as necessary, and only when intimidation failed, unlike some of the hotheads out there. He could be reasoned with, up to a point. As Dot had once told me over drinks: If we must have organized crime, it was better that it be well-organized.

There was a few seconds of just static on the line before Accardo answered. "Okay, you make an acceptable offer.

Those are services I could possibly use. What are you asking for?"

"Just information. Anything you can share about a man called Alex Daubman. I understand he's some kind of high-grade fixer for Mammoth Pictures."

"Yeah, I know about Daubman. We don't cross paths much because our businesses are mostly separate, except maybe when one of Mammoth's stars gets into debt with one of my bookies. He's not just a fixer, he's an enforcer."

"What does that mean?"

"Mostly he just schmoozes and bribes people to make trouble go away. But if bribes don't work, then threats follow. And if threats don't work, then violence comes next. You sure have a way of picking dangerous enemies."

That last was a cold reminder of where we still stood with Accardo.

"I feel like there's something more we should know."

"Yeah, and this is the really valuable bit. Alex Daubman is not his real name. He used to be Lorenzo Vincenti, and he freelanced for the New York Families. He went out west with Bugsy Siegel, but he had to find a new line of work after he cut a deal with the Feds to rat out the Chicago boys when they were moving in on the Hollywood unions. He figured that was New York's territory. Then he changed his name and offered his talents to Mammoth. The Feds wanted to relocate him out of Los Angeles, but he insisted on staying. Says he likes the climate."

"That is well worth knowing," Dot said. "No offense, but I'm surprised somebody from Chicago hasn't bumped him off by now."

"He has the mark of Cain," replied Accardo.

"I don't know what that means," she said. I didn't either. It had never come up in my true crime magazines or even the crime stories I read.

"It means nobody here in Los Angeles will have anything to do with him. But nobody is allowed to get rid of him either, because then there would have to be payback, and soon it would turn into a full-scale war between Chicago and New York. And nobody wants that, least of all over a fink like Daubman. He's under Siegel's protection, but even Siegel doesn't really like him."

Dot was silent for several seconds before speaking again. "If somebody were to take down Daubman legally and your name was nowhere near it, where would we stand?" she asked carefully.

"That person would be in the black in my ledger," he replied. "They would also make a lot of friends in both New York and Chicago. And no enemies, if that's what's worrying you."

"Thanks. I owe you," she said.

"Yes you do," said Accardo, and hung up.

"What was that last part about?" I asked.

"We might have to turn Daubman in before this is over," Dot replied. "I wanted to be sure we're not stirring up an even worse hornet's nest if we do. Anyway, some things are starting to become clearer," said Dot.

"Like how much trouble we're in?" I replied. "We're stuck in the desert with a former mob guy with a violent track record, and no way of getting home without him."

"Let's keep clear heads. For now, Daubman still wants the

same thing we do, to get Helen away from her kidnappers and back to LA. And he has no reason to make a lot of noise by threatening or harming us."

"You're right. So I guess we go along with that, keep what we know to ourselves, and figure out the rest in LA where we're not so isolated."

"Yes. As long as we know more about Daubman than Daubman knows about us, we're at an advantage."

That was Dot's army intelligence experience coming out again.

"Is Daubman going to ask about a long distance call being charged to our room?" I said.

"We'll just tell him we have business in LA and it's confidential," Dot replied.

That only left heading down to the bar to get a drink or two before dinner. I was increasingly tense as we waited for Daubman to arrive, and a beer and a couple of Lucky Strikes were only putting a small dent in my anxiety. He strolled up a little before seven. As usual, he was immaculately dressed, perfectly groomed, and completely creepy. He had the look of a man who assumes that everything he touches belongs to him.

"I have a dinner reservation for the three of us here in the hotel," he said. After what Accardo had told us, I wasn't surprised he didn't have anybody else to eat dinner with.

Sitting at the elegantly set table with its white linen tablecloth and napkins, fine glasses, and silver flatware while next to a mob enforcer felt utterly unreal. All I could think about was what might trigger Daubman to drop his facade, and what it would look like when he did. Was he the kind to fly into a rage, or the coldly calm type?

I was not at all my usual talkative self. Daubman coaxed a stilted story out of me about the time I flew into Las Vegas, but after that, Dot surprised me by prompting him to share some of his Hollywood stories, which kept him talking for the rest of the meal. Like most men of his ilk, he was more than happy to talk about himself, especially if it made him sound rich, famous, or powerful, so he was at the center of most of his yarns. I spent much of the meal hoping he wouldn't try to flirt with either of us. Dot would probably not even notice, but I had no idea how I would handle it.

Finally, relief in the form of coffee arrived and the meal was almost over. Sipping the weak brew, I missed Eddie's café de olla. I glanced over at Dot and wondered if she missed Eddie too. Daubman asked for the check.

I tugged on Dot's sleeve. "I need to fix my lipstick, and it looks like you do too. Come to the restroom with me," I said.

Inside our sanctuary, Dot peered critically at herself in the mirror. It continued to baffle me that she could look at that reflection and not realize how pretty she was.

"My lipstick looks fine. What's wrong with it?" she asked.

"Nothing," I replied. "I just wanted to talk with you privately."

"What about?"

"Daubman. If you hate the show, don't stay. But when you leave, take me with you. I don't think either of us should be alone with him. We really have no idea what he's capable of."

"Of course. And the same goes for you, if you've had all you can take of him."

"How are you handling all this?" I asked. "You look

calm."

"I'm just shutting him out completely," she replied. "It's a handy trick."

We returned to the table and followed Daubman across to the lounge for the show. I'd noticed that he liked to walk a step or two ahead of us, even when we all knew where we were going. It was an annoying habit. I thought about catching up to him to see if he would scurry ahead again, but didn't think it was the best idea to toy with his temper.

A waiter showed us to a table and Daubman insistently arranged us on either side of him. I'd been hoping to position Dot between him and me, but no luck. He ordered a bottle of Champagne. I didn't know whether that was supposed to impress us, or if it was just what he always drank in places like this. I imagined Daubman spending a lot of time sitting in expensive night clubs, with a girl on either side of him and worrying more about the impression he was making than the cost.

The show started promptly at eight and was opened by the chorus line performing the can-can. They were wearing the classic costume, right down to the layers of petticoats and the ridiculous long knickers. I winced. Maybe this had been provocative fun 50 years ago in Paris, but here and now, it was just a cliché, doubly so in this town that had styled itself on Western movie saloons.

The usual vaudeville acts followed for a while, and I noticed that Daubman wasn't very interested. Apparently, he was just here for the girls. I also noticed that he was edging his seat closer to mine while also propping a proprietorial arm across the back of Dot's chair. I shuffled further away as best I could without it being too obvious. Dot seemed completely unaware. That didn't mean she wasn't; she was probably as alert as I was behind her shield. Eventually, the chorus line came out again, this time for some sort of ersatz Broadway show number. Daubman sat up straight, his stare fixed on the high-kicking girls on the stage.

As soon as they were off stage, I turned to Dot. "Can you take me up to our room? I'm getting a headache," I said.

"Are you sure?" said Daubman, before Dot could reply. "They have one more number at the end of the show. It's only another 20 minutes."

"Quite sure," I said. "I think I got too much sun today."

"I'm very tired too," Dot said. "We'll see you at breakfast."

We stood up, collected our purses, and headed for the lobby elevators. Daubman didn't look happy, but I didn't care one jot. We just had to get through one more morning with him.

Chapter Twenty

Dot and I came down for breakfast at around seven. Daubman was already there and waved us over to his table. The waitress poured coffee and took our orders. My heart was pounding merely from sitting next to this man, and I desperately hoped my anxiety wasn't obvious. Dot looked unnaturally calm, but I suspected that underneath, she was as roiled up as I was.

"We'll give it until noon," said Daubman. "I've told the pilots to have the plane prepped and ready, and to file a flight plan."

"So what do people do here for fun during the daytime?" I asked. Not even the casino tables were open yet, and I needed something to keep me moving.

"They start drinking right after breakfast," said Daubman. "This really is not a daytime town."

We finished breakfast and went up to our rooms. It took only a few minutes to pack our bags ready for the return flight. I called the front desk and asked them to send a bell boy to bring the bags down and hold them for us. I hated being so passive. Nothing was in my control. We could only wait on news from Siegel, and failing that, wait for Daubman to be ready to go. Helen had dragged us out here, and I was wondering now if she'd known how dangerous Daubman was when she did that. I wanted to be away from Daubman and alone with Dot. I needed to hear how she was handling this, and if we couldn't act, we needed to at least scheme.

"Let's take a little walk, before it gets too hot," I said.

We stepped outside and I could already feel the day

warming up. That was the thing about the desert: it got hot damn fast, and at night, it would get cold just as fast. We walked up to El Rancho. It had the same Old West theme as The Last Frontier, just like the joints on Fremont Street. Las Vegas was a parody of its own history. We stepped inside and wandered around for a bit, mostly to kill time. There was hardly anything to distinguish it from our hotel: the same bar, the same casino, the same expensive dressing on a cheap building. Nothing here was built to last. With construction on the dam finished, the town had little reason to exist, and it felt like everybody was out to make as much as they could before the boom turned into bust.

We went back outside and strolled slowly down to the building site that was slated to become the Flamingo. It was impressively busy. A large sign in front announced the project as being led by 'William R. Wilkerson', but it was widely rumored that Siegel was the money and the power behind it. Siegel had already been turned away by the city when he tried to get in on Fremont Street, and the story was he was trying to keep his head down on this new venture outside the city limits, so Wilkerson was fronting for him.

We could already see that the footprint was much larger than either El Rancho or The Last Frontier, and the parts of the building that had already gone up confirmed that this was going to be much a bigger affair than anything else in Las Vegas. It felt very different too, like it was built to last.

"It's nice to see something more modern going up," said Dot. "That'll be a nice change from all this mock-Western nonsense."

I looked out across the still-visible foundations of what

would become the swimming pool. "I wonder how many of Siegel's enemies are buried under there," I said.

We stood and watched the construction for a while until the heat and the dust started to get to us. I felt like if I stayed any longer, I'd need to shower again. We walked slowly back to the hotel and, not seeing anything else to do, went to the bar and ordered Cokes.

We'd been sitting in the bar, killing time for about 15 minutes, when Daubman rushed over.

"We've got a lead," he said, slightly breathless. "One of Siegel's guys was at the Arizona Club in Block 16 last night. He caught sight of a girl he liked the look of and asked if she was available. The madam told him the girl didn't work there, and that's when he realized she fit the description and reported back to Siegel."

"Great," I said. "When are we heading over there?"

"I can't take you two in there. It's kind of a seedy place."

"Lisa asked us to come, and we got you this far," I said. "And if she's been treated badly, she'll need taking care of. We're coming."

Daubman chewed his lip for a few seconds. "Okay. I don't like it, but okay."

Daubman had the limo brought around and we climbed in the back. It took us downtown, across to Block 16, and dropped us outside the Arizona Club. He told the driver to wait.

The building was a two story clapboard affair that looked like it could do with repainting. Mind you, that was probably true of anything in this town that wasn't painted last week. From the outside, it looked like any other Las Vegas location with a bar and gambling on the first floor and hotel rooms up above. It was a decent enough cover to run an unlicensed brothel, provided you kept it discreet, paid off the right people, and turned away the soldiers so you didn't upset the Army.

Inside, the place was empty except for a couple of stooped older women sweeping the floor and dusting tables. It had the same basic Western theme as the other places in town, and I found it hard to tell it apart from the others, except for the business upstairs. Next to the stairs was a reception counter for the hotel, and behind it, a door with a frosted glass window. Daubman went over and knocked on the glass and waited. After a few seconds, the door opened on a tall middle-aged woman wearing a long dress and cowboy boots. Her hair was up in a style that seemed very formal for that time of day. Behind her, I could see a desk with cash, some of it sorted into piles.

"I'm sorry," she said to Daubman, "we're not open until seven. The front door should have been locked." She looked at Dot and me standing in the middle of the room. "And we're not hiring," she added.

"We're not here for that. Siegel okayed us coming over," replied Daubman.

"What does he want? As far as I know, we're in good standing."

"There's a girl staying here, but not working. About 5'6", slim, blond hair, blue-green eyes."

"I know the one. I don't know what the deal is with the man she's with, and I'm paid well not to ask about other people's business."

"Siegel wants her gone, and we're here to take her."

She stared at Daubman for several seconds, deciding whether to make a stand on this. Finally, she stepped over to the pegboard of hotel keys and pulled one down.

"Room six," she said. "And try to be quiet. The girls sleep during the day."

We climbed the stairs as quietly as we could and found room six. Daubman unlocked it, turned the handle, and pushed the door open. He got it ajar no more than a foot. A man had grabbed the door and was blocking it from opening any further with his foot.

"What the hell—" the man started to say.

He didn't get anything else out before Daubman's fist smacked into his nose. He went down hard on his rump. Daubman pushed the door fully open and we crowded into the room. The man made to get up, but Daubman immediately stood over him. The man was fat and soft-looking, wearing a stained undershirt and jeans, and no shoes.

"Don't," Daubman said. The man decided he wouldn't.

The room was small, and it felt a lot smaller with all of us trying to get into it. There was a double bed under the window, and sitting on it was Helen. Or Lisa, as I had to keep reminding myself to call her in front of Daubman. Her mouth was hanging open.

"Oh, thank God!" she said. "I had no idea if you would really come for me."

"You two take Lisa downstairs," Daubman said. "I just need to clear some things up with our friend here."

"Just remember what the lady asked," I said. "She said to

keep it quiet."

Lisa scrambled across the bed and followed us out of the room, Daubman pushing the door closed behind us. We were almost at the bottom of the stairs when we heard the shot, followed by a thump. In the morning quiet, the noise filled the whole room and echoed endlessly.

"You two stay here. I'll see what happened," I said. Volunteering to run towards the sound of gunfire was not the smartest thing I'd ever done. Wisely, nobody else offered to go with me.

I was quickly back up to the room, not caring now about the clatter of my shoes on the wooden stairs. I paused for a moment outside to ask myself if I really wanted to do this, then turned the handle and threw the door open. The fat man was lying on his back next to the bed with a small pool of blood spreading across his chest and a much larger one running out from under his body. His eyes were wide open and empty and completely still. I had no doubt he was dead.

Daubman was standing next to the door, holding his pistol. He looked at me and slipped it back into its shoulder holster. "He pulled a gun on me," he said. "I didn't wait for him to shoot."

I looked again and noticed for the first time that a small revolver was lying on the ground near the man's right hand.

"Now what?" I asked.

Daubman stared for a few seconds. "You three take the limo back to the hotel and wait for me there. I need to stay here and straighten this out with Siegel's people."

I turned and went downstairs, grabbed Dot and Helen each by one arm, and propelled them towards the door.

"What happened up there?" asked Dot as I force-marched her and Helen outside.

"Daubman shot that man. He claimed the guy put a gun on him, but he shot first."

"It sounds like you don't believe him?"

"That he drew his gun from his shoulder holster and got a shot away before a guy who already had his gun out and leveled? Not even in the movies. I think he shot the guy in cold blood and then planted a spare gun to sell his story."

"What do we do now?" said Helen. Either she was genuinely scared or a very good actress. I still couldn't make up my mind about her.

"Daubman wants us to go back to the hotel and wait for him. I don't think that's a good idea. I have a nasty feeling that once he has his hands on you, Dot and I become dangerous loose ends."

"I agree. There's a lot of desert out there to lose a couple of bodies in. I want to get as far away from him as possible, as fast as possible," said Dot.

"We need to get out of town, right now," I agreed.

"How though? We don't have a car, and I hope you're not thinking of stealing one. In any case, Daubman will just follow us."

"Nope. I have a better idea. Or a worse one, depending on your point of view," I replied.

We climbed into the waiting limo. The driver was sitting patiently, unfazed. Either he hadn't heard the gunshot, or that kind of thing happened all the time here.

"Back to the hotel?" he asked.

"No," I said. "Alamo Field."

"We're not waiting for Mr. Daubman?"

"He's going to be a while. He said to go ahead."

The drive out to the airfield took twenty minutes, and it was the longest twenty minutes of my life. I spent most of it looking back to see if anybody was following us, and repeatedly thought I'd spotted a tail only to see them turn off a few minutes later.

By the time we got to the airfield, my nerves were shredded. Joy looked about the same. Helen seemed to be preternaturally calm, which I thought might just be her personal reaction to threats. Either that or shock. I hoped she didn't freeze up entirely on us, because physically dragging her through the terminal building was going to attract attention.

"Follow my lead," I told them both. I don't know whether Helen even heard me or was just running on automatic. We crossed the small foyer to the double doors marked General Aviation. Nobody was checking passes or IDs, and nobody looked at us as we went through. There was a small waiting area on the other side, and then another set of doors that led out onto the apron. Marathon's C-47 was sitting out there, the wheels chocked and stairs pulled up to the door. Just like Daubman had asked, it looked ready to go. We started across the apron towards it. Over to my left, I saw a half-dozen ground service workers in overalls and heavy work boots sitting around on luggage carts. I told Joy and Helen to keep going and went over to them.

"Hi boys," I said to them. "Once we're on, can you pull away the stairs and chocks and get us underway? We're ready to go."

"The boss isn't coming?" one of them asked. I guessed Daubman was here often enough that they regularly saw him coming and going.

"No," I said. "He's staying on a few more days. The plane's coming back for him later."

"What about the crew? I didn't see them go on board yet."

"They're getting a few days R and R too. I'm flying her today."

The service worker didn't seem bothered by that, so I assumed he'd seen enough ferry pilots flying into the army base here not to be surprised about a female pilot. I was relieved I didn't have to argue the point.

He waved two of the guys over. They threw down their cigarettes and crushed them under their boots, then walked with me over to the stairs. Dot and Helen were already inside. I scampered quickly up and through the door, closing it behind me as they moved the stairs away. Then I went straight up to the cockpit.

"Dot, I'll need your help," I told her as I passed through the cabin, and she followed me. "Sit there," I said, pointing to the co-pilot seat, "buckle in, and don't touch anything unless I tell you to. Oh, and one more thing. I'll need my sunglasses back."

I adjusted my seat forward a little and got comfortable. I looked the panels over. Nothing was exactly where I was used to seeing it, but it was close enough. All I had to do was get her up and then get her down again later. This should be like my old Bobcat trainer, only bigger, I told myself. Or just like a B-17, but with half as many engines to worry about. I put my Aviators on and smiled.

"Open that window beside you, it slides back," I told Dot. She did so. I peered past her and looked for the guys clearing the chocks. "Okay, now shout 'clear' as loud as you can, then tell me when he gives you a thumbs-up," I said.

"All good," she said.

I primed the starboard engine, got it spinning, let it go for ten blades, then fired it up and throttled back to idle. I repeated the process on the port side, then switched on the radio and called the tower.

"Tower, this is Mammoth Pictures C-47, requesting to bring forward our noon departure, same flight plan as posted."

"Good morning, Mammoth," a crackly voice came back, "Roger that. Go to runway nineteen and then you're clear for immediate takeoff."

"Thank you, tower. What are we looking at up top?"

"Should be unlimited visibility all the way to the coast."

I rolled the plane forward, turned it to face down the runway, and started to throttle up the engines.

"You can fly this?" asked Dot, sounding nervous.

"Probably," I replied. I don't think that was the answer she was hoping for. "We trained on twin engine equipment before they let us handle the big bombers. But I'm not sure what the takeoff speed is on one of these, so it's going to be a lot of touch and feel. Don't worry though, we have plenty of runway. These things were designed to take off from military fields with a full load of cargo."

"What else do you need me to do?"

"I can't reach the handle for the cowl flaps from here, so I'll need you to open them for me, and close them once we get up. It's a simple enough process, and I'll tell you when. It'll also help if you can raise the landing gear when I ask." I pointed out both sets of controls for her.

The radio suddenly came to life again. It was the tower.

"Mammoth Pictures C-47, please hold where you are. There seems to be some discrepancy."

"What's the problem, tower? I'm throttling up and ready to go," I replied.

"There is a man here saying you're not authorized to take that plane."

"Roger that, tower," I said. I turned off the radio and opened up the throttles.

The lightly-loaded plane accelerated rapidly, reminding me of my training days before the heavy bombers. As soon as I felt lift, I nosed up a little and we climbed quickly. Once we had some altitude I pointed us due west, adjusted the trim, and relaxed a little. The controls were light compared to the B-17, and in any case I wouldn't need to touch much as long as we stayed level. I glanced over at Dot, wondering how she was handling her second flight.

"Did we just steal a plane?" said Dot.

"Borrowed," I said.

"What's the difference?"

"Five to ten years, I should think."

"Is this more reckless than breaking into Mammoth studios?"

"Let's call it even. Can you go back and check on Helen, and then come back here? I'm going to need you to navigate a little."

Dot was back in just a couple of minutes.

"She's fine. I told her where to find the bar."

"Can you check that compartment?" I asked. "There should be a chart that covers Las Vegas and Los Angeles."

She rummaged around for a minute. "Got it," she said. She opened it up and refolded it to show everything between us and LA. "What do you need?"

"Look for a town maybe ten miles or so outside LA with enough flat desert to be able to put this bird down. Ideally one near a major highway."

"We're not going back to the air terminal?"

"No, we're not going to fly a stolen plane into an airport. Alamo Field will have been on to every air field west of Las Vegas to warn them to look out for us. We're going to have to finish the journey by road."

"Daubman is going to be right behind us, isn't he?"

"Yes, but unless he can rustle up another plane, he's going to have to follow by car, which should give us several hours' headstart."

Helen poked her head into the cockpit.

"How are you doing?" I asked her.

"Under the circumstances? Okay, I guess. I helped myself to a large Scotch. That's helping."

"That was Logan's people holding you, right?"

"Yes. I'm sorry, I folded, and signed the quitclaim turning it over to them yesterday. I didn't want to, I know it's not really mine, but they threatened to hurt me if I didn't. But they didn't give me my money and they still didn't let me go. I think they were going to kill me."

"How did you get the postcard out? That was clever," said Dot.

"One of the girls took pity on me. I told her a sob story and said my family would be worried if they didn't hear from me, so she promised to smuggle a postcard out for me. Obviously, I had to make the message look harmless."

"That might be the only smart thing you've done since I met you."

"When we get back to LA, we have to put this whole business to rest. You, Daubman, Logan, all of it. Nobody is safe until we are rid of that cursed property," I said.

"But I already signed it over to Logan."

"Legally, that's not worth the paper it's written on," said Dot. "A quitclaim just turns over your rights to the property, and you never had any. Once Logan figures out who you really are, he's going to realize his title is no good."

"But how will he find out?"

"You're going to have to tell him. Until you do, he's going to consider you a loose end that needs cleaning up."

Her face dropped. She turned and went back to the cabin, probably for another Scotch.

Dot returned to her map reading. "Okay, I see a place called Palmdale. It's not as close to LA as you asked for, but once you get past there, everything turns to forest, so I think that's as good as it gets. It looks like there's a decent road to LA nearby, Route 6."

"Can you figure out a heading?" I asked.

"How fast are we going?" she asked.

"200 knots." She looked blank. "Uh, 230 miles an hour. And we've been flying due west since we left."

She stared at the map for a minute. "Right. Keep on this course another 50 minutes, then turn to the south-west, and hopefully you'll be able to see it ahead of us after twenty minutes more, right before we reach the forest."

"Did you just do that in your head?" I asked.

"Yes, it's really not that hard to figure a rough heading. Of course, you'll have to adjust for wind yourself. Now if you don't need me, I'm going in the back to get a drink too."

That left me an hour or so to figure out how to play our hand when we got back to LA. There had to be an end to this.

Dot's navigation was good enough under the circumstances. Palmdale came into sight off to port and I circled over a couple of times, looking for somewhere to land. We'd overshot the desert and it was mostly farmland, and I spotted a large field that looked fallow. It wasn't ideal, but these planes were supposed to be tough. Time to find out. I yelled to Joy and Helen to strap themselves in as best they could. I brought us in as low and slow as I dared, and then eased her down. We hit and bounced, then came back down hard. The landing gear held up, thankfully. I heard glass breaking back in the cabin, and assumed I'd just spilled a lot of liquor. The wheels stuck the second time, and the plane bumped and bounced and rolled to a stop at the end of the field, its nose poking over a fence at a field full of incurious cows. I sat back and took a few deep breaths and hoped my heart would stop pounding soon. It was the worst landing of my life, and I was glad none of my instructors had witnessed it.

I went back and checked on Joy and Helen. They were both shaken but unhurt. I opened the door and looked down. There was a drop of about four or five feet without stairs to climb down. I sat down on the edge then scooted over and dropped to the ground. Dot and then Helen followed me down. We trudged to the road. A mile marker confirmed it was Route 6.

"What now?" said Helen.

"Now we start walking, and hope for a lift," I replied.

It wasn't as hot here as out in the desert, but it was plenty hot enough. Every step kicked up dust off the road that attached itself to our sweat. I realized how foolish we'd been not to look for bottled water on the plane. The only grace note was that the sun was almost overhead and not in our eyes, although it would be if we kept walking long enough. My feet ached, but I couldn't imagine how Dot's felt. Her heels were not designed for going any distance on a road like this one.

We'd been walking about 45 minutes when a beat-up truck with an open bed came by and stopped for us. It might have been blue at one time, but it was hard to tell now.

"How much for a ride to LA?" I asked.

The driver, an old hispanic man with salt-and-pepper hair, looked us over. We must have looked a mess. He didn't ask why, which had always seemed to be the way with country folk when I was growing up.

"All three of you, 30 bucks," he said. "And I'll throw in the water." He patted the cooler on the bench seat next to him. "You'll all have to ride in the back, though. My dog has the front seat." On cue, a collie sat up, stuck its head out the window, and hung its tongue out.

We were dirty, thirsty, exhausted, and on the run from a mob killer. Thirty bucks was a bargain. We clambered in the back, arranged some empty sacks to sit on, and braced ourselves as best we could.

Chapter Twenty-One

An hour later, we were dropped off in front of our office, tired and dehydrated. Our butts were bruised and our bodies were stiff, but we were relieved to be back. Unfortunately, we had no idea how far—or how little—ahead of Daubman we were.

Dot and I exchanged a glance, and each took one of Helen's arms.

"What's this?" she said, struggling to free herself.

"No more running off," I told her. "We have to settle things for good."

We steered her inside and I locked the door behind us. We went through to the back and I locked the office door too, then we sat her down in a chair in front of my desk and I sat down behind it. Dot busied herself making coffee, which we all desperately needed. I thought about the bottle of Scotch in my bottom drawer, but that would have to wait. Business first. So I reached into the top drawer, pulled out my sap, and put it on the desk in front of me.

"Don't even think about doing anything stupid," I told her.

She sagged. All the energy, fight and defiance had gone out of her. It finally seemed like she was done running. Dot put coffee in front of us and took hers to her own desk.

I picked up my phone and started dialing, and signaled Dot to pick up her extension too.

"Who are you calling?" said Helen.

"Detective Ramirez. You met him at my father's apartment."

"Why?"

"You're going to turn yourself in. Your best chance, maybe your only chance now, is to testify against Daubman, and Logan too. There's just a possibility the cops will believe you were a patsy in all this, and the only thing you'll be guilty of is the attempted fraud with the deed."

She half-rose from her chair. I paused my dialing.

"Try to tough it out and you could end up taking the fall for my father's death," I added. "They don't often send women to the gas chamber in this state, but it happens."

She sat down again.

"Will I go to prison?"

"Probably," I said. "It depends what else is on your record. But think about the alternative."

I dialed the last few digits. Eddie picked up.

"Hey ace, it's Joy and Dot," I said.

"Where have you two been?" he said. "It's like you dropped off the edge of the planet the last two days. I was worried. And you've missed a whole lot."

"We have a lot for you too. Can we go first?"

"Sure."

I gave him the short version of our trip to Las Vegas and our unconventional return, with Dot filling in the details I missed. He expressed disbelief and disapproval in all the right places, some of it in language that Dot didn't like to hear. It was probably for the best that she didn't understand cussing in Spanish.

"Anyway, Helen wants to come in and cut a deal. She'll give up both Daubman and Logan. How's that sound?"

"That's great. I'll send a car right over."

"Okay, what do you have for us?"

"First up, good news about Daubman. After Lisa—uh, Helen, I guess—was kidnapped, my Detective-three agreed there was something bigger going on, and he let me reopen the Tony D'Amico case and get some forensics done. You're going to like what we found, but I don't want to spoil the surprise for you.

"We wanted to bring Daubman in for questioning and his office told us he'd taken the company plane to Las Vegas, so we asked the local PD to watch for him there. After the shooting, Siegel put him on the first commercial flight out of town, before the local cops even knew what had happened. Luckily, they gave us a heads up once they heard the news, and we picked him up at the air terminal at this end."

"What will happen with the shooting? Will he be charged back in Las Vegas?" asked Dot.

"It probably depends on Siegel. I hear he swings a lot of weight in that town. If Siegel likes Daubman, he'll find some mook to swear under oath he saw the other guy pull first. If Seigel wants rid of Daubman, he'll arrange for it to go the other way. The cops out there won't ask too many questions. They don't care about mobsters killing mobsters, as long as civilians don't get hurt and it doesn't scare off the tourists."

Eddie sounded very casual about it, as if this kind of premeditated miscarriage of justice was routine when dealing with the Mob.

"Where's Daubman now?" I asked.

"He's cooling his heels in a cell right now, and refusing to say anything until his lawyer gets here," replied Eddie.

"Wow, that's a huge relief," I said.

"Absolutely," added Dot.

"The news about Logan isn't quite as good. Thanks to the license plate Dot gave us, we now know who Logan is. He's Paul Logan, an executive with the City of Angels Oil Company."

Suddenly things started to come into focus.

"If there's oil under that lot…" I started to say. There was oil all over LA, and in Beverly Hills too. After you had lived here a while, you got used to seeing derricks in random places in the middle of a block or next to a high school. New finds turned up from time to time, and the rights were promptly fought over.

"Yeah, then it's worth a whole lot more than the 10,000 Logan and Daubman have been kicking around," said Eddie. "It could be as much as a million, depending on how much is down there. Maybe that's enough to make some people think it was worth killing for."

I whistled. "And no wonder they wanted to avoid a bidding war over it, if they could get it cheap."

I looked over at Helen, but she was stony-faced.

"Also, we found the two goons who snatched James," continued Eddie. "Believe it or not, they were still driving the same stolen car. A couple of Highway Patrolmen spotted it outside a roadhouse on the PCH. The two of them were inside, happily drinking beer when the patrolmen picked them up."

"These are not the smartest people, are they?" said Dot.

"Nope. Anyway, when we explained to them that kidnapping across a state line could get them twenty years in

Federal prison, they quickly rolled over on Logan."

"That's great too, but it sounds like there's also bad news," I said.

"Yeah, we still haven't picked up Logan himself. His secretary claims she doesn't know where he is. He might have gotten a tip-off and gone to ground."

We were all silent over that for a moment.

"I have an idea how to maybe flush him out," I said. "It's a little bit dangerous, but it might wrap this situation up once and for all. What are you doing tonight, say around six?"

"Is this for work, or for a date with Dot?" said Eddie.

I deserved that.

"Work," I said and explained my idea. "I'll bet his secretary knows how to reach him. I'll call her up, tell her I want to meet him to sell him the deed because this is all too hot for me to handle. I'll arrange the meet somewhere you can safely get the jump on him. What do you think?"

"You're right," said Eddie. "That is dangerous. Are you sure you want to do that?"

"I don't want to go around looking over my shoulder for Logan for the rest of my life," I replied. "This is better."

"Okay, I guess. Do you have a place in mind?"

"There's a park near here. It'll be empty after the stores close, so you'll have open lines of sight and no civilians to worry about."

"So while you're meeting with him, where am I? I can't be in the open in the park."

"Sitting in your car," I replied.

"That won't work, it's obviously a cop car, even without the markings. It'll scare him off."

Eddie was right. I thought for a few seconds. "I have an idea. Come by the store. I'll get us a car that'll be inconspicuous."

After we hung up, Dot looked across at me. "Are you going to borrow a taxi?" she asked.

"No, much better," I smirked. I picked up the phone and called Ginnie.

When I was done, I looked over at Helen.

"Did you know about the oil?"

"Not at first," she said wearily. "I thought it was just a scrap of land Mammoth or Twentieth might want to buy. But after Logan and Wetherby came to me with an offer that seemed way too generous, I figured it out."

"And that's when you demanded more from Daubman?"

"Yes. I reckoned Mammoth would pay a lot more to avoid having oil derricks churning away right next to their backlot."

"Yeah, I can see that the noise and the smell would be a problem for movie productions."

"I still don't get what Daubman's angle was," said Dot. "It doesn't make sense that he was willing to kill to save Mammoth some money."

Helen turned to face her. "Daubman knew about the oil the whole time. That's why he'd been using Mammoth's money to make the property tax payments. I was supposed to sell to him for what the land was worth by itself, because I didn't know any better. And then he was going to demand a whole lot more from Mammoth to sell the property to them, or he'd sell out to an oil company."

"And for that, he killed three people," I said softly.

We all sat quietly after that and finished our coffee while

we waited for the patrol car to pick up Helen.

Once she was gone, I picked up the phone again. I dialed Logan's office. His secretary answered.

"Mr. Logan's office, how can I help you?"

"I need to speak with Mr. Logan," I said.

"I'm afraid he's not in the office right now, and nobody knows where he is."

"Yeah, but I bet you know how to get a message to him, if it's important enough."

The silence that followed was very loud.

"I thought so," I continued. "Tell him it's Joy, and I can wreck his deal with Lisa. If he still wants the property, he needs to call me urgently. I want to get paid. He'll know what all that means."

There was more silence. "Very well," she finally said, and hung up on me.

Now it was just a matter of waiting again. I settled down with some detective magazines. After an hour, the phone rang. It was Logan.

"What are you trying to pull?" he said angrily. "Lisa signed the quitclaim. The lot is legitimately mine now."

"Yeah, but that deal ain't worth the paper it's written on."

"What do you mean?"

"Lisa is a phony. An imposter. The real Lisa D'Amico died 18 years ago. There's a death certificate on file."

There was a long pause. "So why are you calling me?"

"With Lisa out of the picture, I'm the sole owner of the property. Lucky for you, I want out of this whole mess, and I'd rather sell to the kidnapper than the murderer."

"What are you proposing?"

"I'll meet you and sign over the property. I want 100,000."

"A hundred grand? What makes you think it's worth that?"

"I know about the oil. Ten percent of the value seems fair to me. Better bring a company check, because I don't want to be walking around with that much cash."

"Where and when?"

"Somewhere I'll feel safe. In the open. There's a park not far from my office, with a tree in the middle surrounded by benches. Be there at six, on the north side of the tree. If everything looks legit, I'll come over and we'll get it done right there. If anything looks wrong to me, I'll walk away and I'll find another buyer." I gave him the location of the park and hung up.

I called Eddie back and then Ginnie. "We're on," I told each of them.

Exhaustion hit me. "I wish we had a couch," I said to Dot. I leaned back in my chair and dozed fitfully. When I woke, I barely felt more rested. I was running on coffee and adrenaline.

Eddie arrived around 5:30 p.m. and Dot and I met him outside. He was right about the car; the big spotlight and the antenna for the two-way radio were obvious giveaways. A few minutes later, Ginnie pulled up in her midnight blue two-door Caddie 62 Coupe.

Eddie stared. "You and I have very different understandings of the word 'inconspicuous'," he said eventually.

Ginnie slid out and I made the introductions. "Ginnie, this is Detective Eddie Ramirez, he's the lead investigator on this case. Eddie, this is our friend and financial backer,

Ginnie Townsend."

"Nice to meet you, and I promise to take very good care of your car," Eddie said to Ginnie.

"Hold on a second," Ginnie replied. "Nobody but me drives this car. I didn't even let my chauffeur behind the wheel except to pull it out of the garage to wash it."

"I understand how you feel. It's a beautiful car," said Eddie, "but this is a police operation and it could get dangerous."

"Too dangerous for me sitting next to you, but not too dangerous for Joy out there by herself?" she replied. It was an excellent point, and Eddie threw up his hands in surrender.

"Just be sure to park on the expensive side of the street and nobody will question the car," I told Ginnie.

Ginnie and Eddie left to get the car in position. Around 5:45 p.m., Dot and I left the office and walked towards the park. The sun was low in the west, but there was still enough daylight. Sunset was more than an hour away. A block from the park, we stopped.

"I'll go alone from here," I told Dot.

"Are you really sure about this?" she asked me anxiously.

"I'm sure. Wait for me at the station. I'll see you there when this is done."

She didn't look happy, but she nodded, turned back, and walked towards the streetcar stop.

I walked on and turned right into the park. A hundred feet or so away, sitting next to the tree, Logan was waiting where I'd told him to. I crossed the grass and sat down next to him.

"Do you have the paperwork?" I asked.

"No," he replied. I raised my eyebrows. He pulled his hand out from under his coat and pushed an automatic pistol hard into my ribs. If I could have raised my eyebrows any higher, I would have.

"There's no more deals for me. The Feds want me on kidnapping charges, but before I go on the lam, I'm going to make you pay for ruining me."

I didn't make you kidnap Helen, I thought, but decided to keep that to myself.

"Get up and walk," he continued, "up to the street. Don't make a fuss, don't make a noise. I don't want to kill you here, but I will if you make me."

We walked north, his gun still poking me. His strangler's fingers gripped the back of my neck tight enough to bruise, in case I tried to pull away. He's going to choke me, I thought, and he's going to enjoy it. We stepped from the grass onto the street and walked over to his car. He took me around to the passenger side and told me to open the door.

"Get in and slide over under the wheel," he told me. "I can't drive and hold a gun on you at the same time, so you're driving."

I shuffled under the wheel and he climbed in after me, keeping his pistol pointed at me the whole time.

"Drive east and I'll tell you where to turn," he said. "Keep it nice and careful and under the speed limit. If you do something to make the cops pull us over, I'll shoot you right there and take my chances."

I pulled away from the curb easily. There was almost no traffic at that time of the evening. I made a textbook stop at the next intersection, and pulled away gently.

"Smooth. You're going to go three more blocks and then make a right."

I put my turn signal on nice and early, and turned on the headlights.

"What did you do that for?" he said, sitting up, suddenly alert.

"It's twilight already," I said. "I don't want to forget later and get us stopped for no lights."

He relaxed back a little, at least as much as I'd guess a man holding a hostage before going on the run from the Feds could relax.

I checked my rearview mirror. The car behind me also had its headlights on. It was a block back. I hoped it was Ginnie and Eddie. I took my time at the next stop sign, letting it get closer.

"What are you waiting for?" said Logan impatiently, poking me again. "Let's go."

Suddenly I pulled the hand throttle out as far as it would go and took my foot off the brake. The car lurched forward, throwing Logan back in his seat, his gun pointing up in the air.

"What the hell?" he yelled.

I threw the wheel hard to the right and he rolled against the passenger door. His gun fell loose and dropped into the footwell. I wrenched the wheel back to the left, flicked open the door handle, and tumbled out of the car. The hand throttle kept the car accelerating as it jumped the curb and slammed hard into a telephone poll.

I rolled over and tried to pick myself up as quickly as I could. I was winded, my shoulder burned, my hands were scraped, and I thought I might have broken a rib, but all that would have to wait for later. I just hoped Logan was having a rougher ride than I was. My purse lay open at my side. I pulled out my Detective Special, came up to one knee, and pointed it towards the car. The passenger door opened and Logan stumbled out like a drunk man. He came around the car, his gun in his hand again.

"Drop it, Logan!" I yelled in the firm command voice my gun instructor had taught us, the one you used when you hoped you didn't have to use your gun. Logan just grimaced and leveled his gun at me.

"Don't do anything stupid!" I bellowed.

He smirked and cocked the hammer of his gun, and I did the same. At that instant, Ginnie's Caddie screamed to a halt, brakes squealing, the bitter-sweet smell of scorched tires filling the air. The car was still rocking on its springs as the passenger door opened. Eddie stepped out, his service revolver drawn. He kept the car door between him and Logan as he put his gun on Logan.

"Don't do anything stupid, Mr. Logan," he said.

I risked a quick glance at Eddie. "I just said that!" I shouted.

Logan swung his gun from me to Eddie and back to me. The silence was endless. He grinned like a madman and I thought he was going to take the crazy way out. Then he froze. I heard Ginnie's voice from behind him.

"The gun poking you in the back is small, but it's enough to mess up your guts. Please lower your gun and put an end to this nonsense," she said with remarkable calm.

Logan looked like he was still thinking about firing for a

long second, but then he carefully lowered his gun to the floor and raised his hands.

I waited while Eddie cuffed him and put him in the back of Ginnie's car. My heartbeat and breathing were slowly returning to normal, but my body was still burning with adrenaline. I felt fairly sure I was going to hurt all over once it wore off.

"That's not how that was supposed to go," I said to Eddie. "What happened to taking him at the tree?"

"When I realized he had a gun on you, I didn't want to do anything that might make him panic. We couldn't even start to follow until you turned the corner."

"Well, I'm glad you got here in the end."

"That was a good idea turning on the tail lights, it made it a lot easier for me to pick you out. Are you hurt, by the way?"

"I'll have bruises later, but that's all," I lied. My flight jacket was scuffed, and my pants were torn. My left shoulder, left hip, ribs, and back all ached badly, but I wasn't about to admit that jumping out of a moving car wasn't my most brilliant move ever.

I turned to Ginnie. "I didn't know you carried a gun."

"What gun?" she replied. She opened her hand. She was holding a tube of lipstick.

Ginnie drove us back to the station and I sat alongside her, nursing my bruises. Eddie sat in the back so he could keep his gun on Logan. Even handcuffed, he didn't trust a desperate man. At the station, a couple of uniforms took Logan off our hands for booking and Eddie led Ginnie and me upstairs to his desk where Dot was waiting for us as patiently as ever. She opened her eyes wide when she saw the state of my clothes.

"What the heck happened?" she asked.

"It's fine," I said, "I'll tell you all about it over drinks. And we got Logan."

"Come on upstairs," said Eddie. "I'm going to question Daubman. You'll enjoy this."

He led us up to the interrogation rooms, and showed us into the observation room. There were a couple of men in there already. Eddie's superiors, I guessed. At the table, Daubman sat with his right hand handcuffed to the table. He was still wearing his suit from that morning, minus the tie and the cufflinks. I couldn't see his feet, but I suspected they had taken his shoelaces away too. It was the scruffiest I had ever seen him. Next to him sat a tall, thin, balding man in a conservatively cut black suit, who was presumably his lawyer. Eddie entered with a leather briefcase in his hand and sat down across from them. He set the briefcase on the table, flicked the locks open, pulled out a manilla folder and a notebook. He arranged them neatly in front of himself. It was good theater.

"Mr. Daubman, we're ready to charge you with a number of offenses, including the murder of Tony D'Amico," said Eddie.

"You've got nothing on me, because I didn't do it," said Daubman. He was doing his best to look confident.

"We have a witness who will testify that the whole thing was your idea, and that you threatened her into cooperating with you."

"The Lisa D'Amico woman? She's a serial liar and a

fraudster. I don't think her word's going to carry much weight with a jury."

"You're probably right. Fortunately, we also have physical evidence."

Daubman maintained his poker face. "That's impossible," he said.

"I admit," said Eddie, "you did do a good job of wiping down D'Amico's room. We couldn't even find his prints on the door handles, let alone yours. But you missed the one place you couldn't reach."

Now Daubman was looking worried. "What do you mean?"

Eddie pulled a bag from inside his briefcase and tipped its contents onto the table. Landing with a resounding thud, it was one half of the belt that had hanged my father.

"The inside of the knot you tied in D'Amico's belt. We got some very good prints from there. I guess hanging a man is sweaty work."

Daubman jumped to his feet, but was pulled up short by his handcuffs. His lawyer tugged on his sleeve and he sat down again. He looked very pale now.

Daubman's lawyer leaned over to him and muttered something in his ear. Daubman nodded weakly with his eyes fixed on the table.

"We'd like to discuss a plea deal," said the lawyer.

Chapter Twenty-Two

Friday was completely dead, and for once, I was grateful. Everywhere that hurt yesterday hurt more today. My shoulder and hip had stiffened up so I was lurching more than walking, and every part of my back that I could see in the mirror was turquoise and green. Dot and I did paperwork and read and drank coffee and smoked, and talked over the events of the past two weeks, trying to get them out of our system. We took a long lunch and came back to the office, finally starting to feel like some sort of normality was returning. I even dozed a little in my chair.

Four o'clock came around and we agreed we deserved to close up early. I wanted to head over to Jack's and wait for the cab drivers to show up so I could share all the news, and Dot planned to head home and get changed for a date with Eddie. We opened the front door, stepped out, and stopped short.

Helen was standing right outside.

"This is a surprise," I said. "And not a pleasant one. I didn't think I'd see you again."

"I know," she replied. "But I didn't want to leave everything the way we had when we parted. Now that the truth is out and you're going to get what's due to you, there's no reason for us to disagree anymore."

"There's also no reason for us to see each other anymore," I countered.

"Well, no. But I still wanted to thank you properly. I owe you. You took risks for me I didn't deserve. If not for you and Dot, I probably would have gotten myself killed in this stupid business. Or locked up for life. As it is, they're probably going to put me away for a while, though I'll get some time off for cooperating over Logan and Daubman."

She sounded genuinely chastened. I reminded myself not to trust appearances.

"Well, you almost got me killed, so that's probably true," I told her.

"Can I come inside and thank you in person, and say a proper goodbye?"

I paused for a few seconds. "Inside? I'm not sure about that."

"Please. It would mean a lot to me. And it'd allow me to draw a line under this whole business. And I want to give you a small gift."

I paused again, still wary. "Okay, I guess so…"

Dot looked at me, her brow furrowed in worry. "Are you sure this is a good idea?" she asked.

"It will be fine. I still have some questions of my own that I'd like answered."

"Do you want me to stay?"

"Nah, you go on ahead. Have fun with Eddie. If it makes you feel better, I promise to have my gun and my sap close at hand, just in case."

Helen tilted her head, perhaps unsure whether or not I was joking.

Dot still didn't look too happy, but she sighed and nodded. "You're a lot more forgiving than I would be under the circumstances," she said.

For once, I didn't want her to Big Sister me.

I led Helen inside and through to the office. We sat across my desk from each other, just as we had the first day we'd met. The stiff primness she had presented before was gone. She was slumped and hunched and worn. She looked like she'd aged five years in the last few weeks. I tugged open the top drawer of my desk. My gun and my sap sat there, in easy reach. I still didn't trust her.

She pulled a pint of Scotch from her purse. "Do you have glasses?" she asked.

I stared at her, disbelieving. "I don't think I should drink from your bottle. You have a bit of track record as far as that goes," I said sardonically.

She sighed. "I understand," she said. "If it makes you feel better, I'll take the first shot."

I opened the bottom drawer, pulled out a couple of shot glasses and set them in the middle of the desk. She unscrewed the bottle and poured two measures. I watched closely as she downed hers, making sure she swallowed, then refilled her glass. Still wary, I picked mine up and sipped.

"The police let you out then," I said.

"Yes. They only charged me with the fraud, and put everything else on Logan in return for my testimony. I'm out on bail until the trial. "

"I guess they figure Daubman is an easier conviction for the killings."

"Do you forgive me?" she asked.

"Absolutely not!" I almost shouted. I took a breath to calm myself before continuing. "Because of your little scam, I've been thrown around, kidnapped, threatened, and I've had guns pointed at me more than once. And you almost stole what little inheritance I have. But once you're gone, I'll try to forget you."

"Okay, I'll settle for that," she said. She took a sip from her glass, and I drained mine. She refilled my glass and topped off her own.

"I'm genuinely sorry about it all. And I really do want to thank you, though. You helped me when you didn't have to, and even when you thought I might be trying to steal from you."

I drained my glass a second time, and she filled it again. I drank half of it just as quickly while she sipped at hers. I was still close to boiling inside. Something about seeing her sitting in front of me instead of behind bars made me want to drink. "Yeah, well, don't kid yourself that was about you. I thought the people coming after you were even worse than you were. Even when I knew you were running a con, I didn't think you deserved to die over it."

I realized that I had slurred the last part of that.

"Are you feeling okay?" said Helen, her head tilted to the side.

"What...?" I said, my thoughts muddled. I struggled to focus on Helen, fighting against the weight of my eyelids. Surely I hadn't drunk that much. She was smiling. No, smirking. I reached for my glass one more time and only succeeded in knocking it over, spilling Scotch across the desk. She was grinning now.

"Did you... did you drug me?" I muttered. My tongue felt too thick to talk.

I reached for the drawer with my gun and sap, but my arm was too heavy and I could only grab its edge. I slumped out of my chair and pulled the drawer down on top of me. Then everything went cloudy and dark.

I was walking through a dense fog, and my head kept spinning, dragging my body around. Up ahead, there was a red light and I walked towards it. Slowly it got bigger, but it was just a red blur. I realized I was waking up, and opened my eyes. I immediately closed them again and turned my head away from the angle lamp shining directly in my face. My mouth felt like it was full of gauze and I worked my jaw to get some spit moving.

"I'm sorry about that," said Helen out of the darkness behind the lamp, and pointed it away from me. "I was just trying to get you to come around. You've been out for an hour or so, you know, and I was getting impatient."

"What the hell?" I mumbled through uncooperative lips. "You drugged me!"

"Yes, I did, didn't I?"

"But how? We drank from the same bottle." I shook my head, trying to clear some of the muzziness.

"I thought that was quite clever, actually. I swallowed charcoal before I came here, it absorbs the barbiturates very well. The booze too. And I only drank one glass to your three. I was actually a little dopey for about twenty minutes myself, but I helped myself to your coffee and I'm wide awake now. I know you don't think I'm very smart, but I'm really very good at certain things."

Somehow, she'd gotten me up into my chair, and my hands were tied in front of me. My ankles were tied too. My gun and my sap were on the desk, out of my reach. Outside of the glare of the angle lamp, the rest of the office was completely in shadow. I shook my head again, hoping the cobwebs would fall away.

"I don't get it. What's this about? You can't still think you can get a payoff."

"Revenge," she said. "That's all. I had one shot at a big payday, and you ruined it for me. I'll never see the money, but this way, neither will you."

"Be smart, Helen. You think you can get away with murder? Or should I say, another murder?"

"Oh, you figured that out? Well done. Yes, I killed Wetherby. He was going to get Tony's quitclaim annulled to avoid paying for it, and I couldn't allow that."

"What about Tony? You kill him too?"

"I drugged him, and forged the paperwork. The rest was all Daubman's work, although I did put him up to it."

"And the black eye? Did Daubman really hit you?"

"Did you like that? Stage make-up. I guessed you see a lot of wives whose husbands hit them in this business, so I thought it would appeal to you."

"What now?" I asked. I was stalling for time to try to clear my head, and I was running out of stalls.

She picked up my revolver which had been sitting on the desk. "Now I'm going to shoot you in the head with your own gun," she said icily. "Then I'll untie you. It will look like suicide. I'm sure people will wonder why, but you never really know what's in another person's mind, do you?"

She flipped open the cylinder and checked it was loaded. "It's been a very bad year for the D'Amico family and suicide, hasn't it?" she said.

"You killed Emma too, didn't you?"

"Yes. I was done taking care of her and getting nothing in return. The bitch was going to live forever."

My anger was burning off the mental fog, but I didn't see anything I could do. I struggled with the ties around my hands but they wouldn't budge.

"You won't win," I said. It was a horrible cliché and I really hoped it wouldn't be my last words. I was just saying desperate things to keep her talking. "Dot will figure it out and come after you. Eddie will come after you. You'll never have peace."

She came around the desk and crouched down to look at me face to face, the gun hanging down by her side. "It will be Monday before anybody finds you. By then, I'll be in another city living under a different name." She put her face so close to mine I could feel her breath. "I don't need peace. I just need to settle the score."

I bobbed my head back and smashed my forehead forward into her nose as hard as I could. The chair rocked backwards with the force of the impact. I felt a satisfying crunch. She howled in pain and dropped the gun to clutch her face. It skittered under the desk.

I kicked her hard in the knee cap and my chair slid back as she yelled again and went down. I rolled off the chair, onto the floor, under the desk, and came up the other side holding the gun in both hands, ignoring the screaming protests from my bruises. I pointed the gun at her chest.

She grabbed the side of the desk and slowly pulled herself to her feet, trying to keep her weight off of her damaged leg.

Her face was ugly with rage. "Sit down on the floor or I'll shoot you," I told her, as calmly as I could manage.

She grimaced through the pain. "No you won't," she grimaced. She stepped around the desk.

I cocked the hammer.

"I bet you've never shot somebody before. It's harder than it looks," she said, taking another step forward. She was just two paces away from me now.

I squeezed the trigger and shot her through the right shoulder. She screamed even louder than before and staggered backwards.

"Sit down on the floor or I'll shoot you in the leg next," I said.

Sobbing heavily, she did as she was told, and lowered herself as carefully as she could. She sat there looking down, her tears and snot mingling as she pressed her blouse against her wound to try to stop the bleeding. I pulled the phone across the desk to myself. I lifted the receiver, heard the dial tone, and put it down on the desk. I clumsily dialed the number of the Belvedere, picked up the receiver again, spoke briefly to the desk clerk, and then waited a few moments. A familiar gravelly voice came on.

"Sam?" I said. "I'm glad you're still there. I'm over at the office and I could use a little help. Can you sit on somebody for me until the police come?"

"No problem," he said. "I'll be there in ten minutes."

He was as good as his word.

Chapter Twenty-Three

It was three o'clock the following Tuesday and Dot, Ginnie, and I were in the lounge of the Marmont, drinking cocktails. Ginnie was trying to teach me to like Rob Roys. Dot and I had spent the best part of an hour explaining the whole tangled story for her, answering every question we could. Considering it was her money that was backing our business, it was the least we could do in return.

"What about the airplane? Are you going to be in trouble for taking it?" she asked me.

"No, there's good news there too," I said. "Mammoth is deeply embarrassed that they'd been employing a mobster who has now been charged with murder in two states. They really don't want any more publicity about that if they can avoid it. They've agreed to forget the whole thing in return for us promising not to talk to the press about it."

"And what about you? Now this is all settled, I assume you'll sell the lot. Do I need to teach you how to behave like an oil heiress?"

"You know, there's one thing everybody has been overlooking this whole time," I said. "Even Dot."

They both looked at me quizzically.

"Tony never divorced my mother. So his marriage to Emma wasn't valid. Even if Helen had legitimately been Lisa D'Amico, she wouldn't have had a claim to the lot. And I don't either. The property belongs to my mother, and always did. She's the next of kin. The whole business with Helen was a charade from start to finish."

A charade that got three people killed, I reflected. And I

was almost the fourth.

Dot was quiet for a moment while she sipped her cocktail and took that in. "Mind you, it's going to be complicated to get all the paperwork sorted out and the probate executed and the title reverted to her," she said.

"My lawyer can help with that," said Ginnie. "He lives for that kind of thing. He'll be happy as a clam for months."

"And when that's all done, Mammoth and Twentieth can bid for the property," I said. "LA has enough oil wells."

"What do you think your mother will do with the money?" asked Dot.

"Knowing her, she'll pay off the mortgage on the farm. Then she'll buy a new farm truck, and carry on as if nothing has changed."

"And one day, eventually, you'll inherit the farm and be modestly rich. What will you do then?"

"I'll quit the P.I. business and take up farming," I said, grinning mischievously.

"And in the meantime?" asked Ginnie.

"In the meantime, I'm going to learn to like Rob Roys. Let's have another round."

ABOUT THE AUTHOR

J.T. Berry has carefully avoided the kinds of jobs and adventures that make authors sound interesting in these biographies, apart perhaps from that one time in Czechoslovakia. After a first career that involved lots of office cubicles and slide presentations, J.T. is now attempting to make a living as a writer. This is the second book in the D'Amico and Stone mystery series.

9 7 9 8 9 9 1 0 7 2 7 8 6